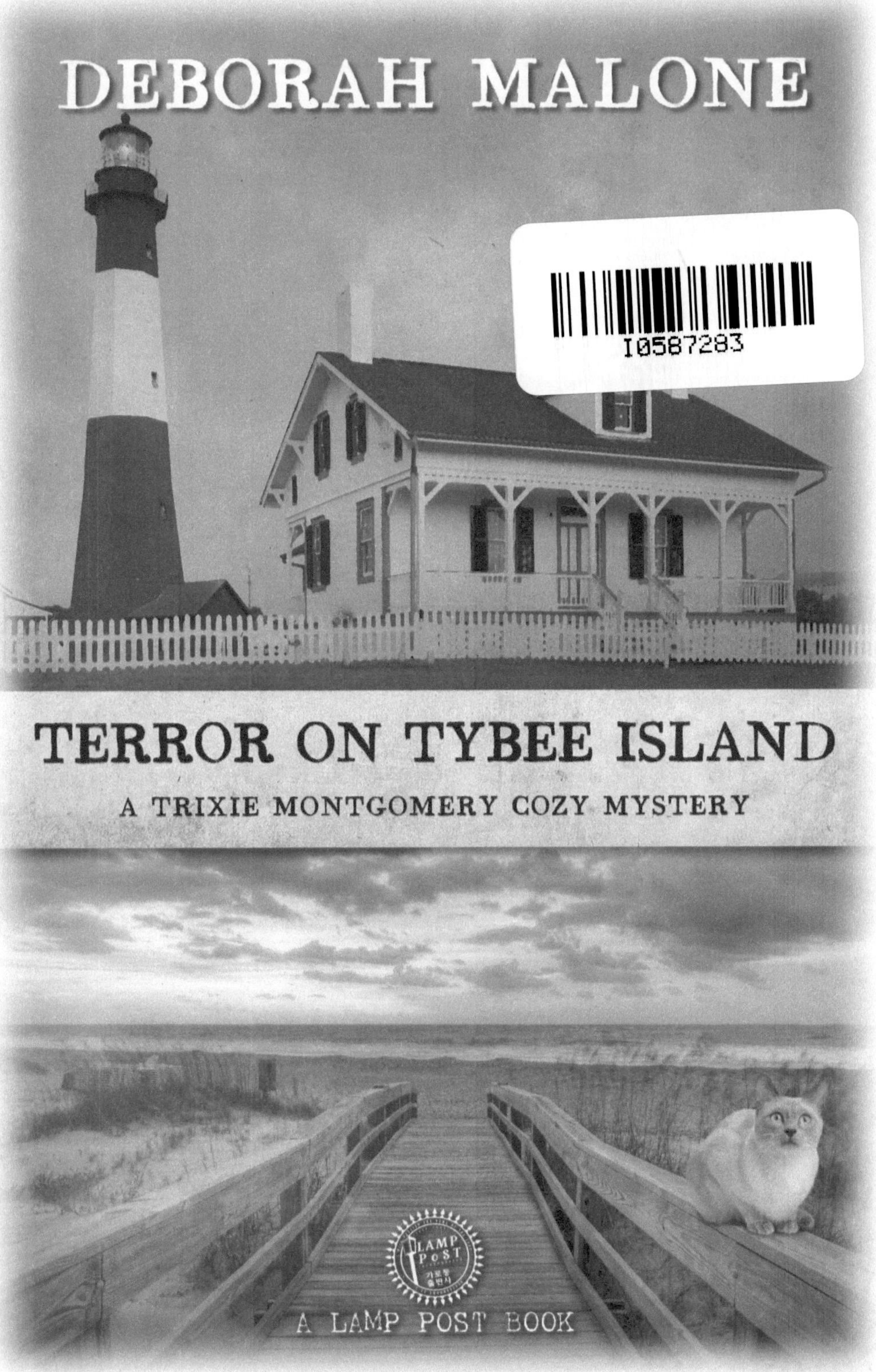
DEBORAH MALONE
TERROR ON TYBEE ISLAND
A TRIXIE MONTGOMERY COZY MYSTERY
LAMP POST
A LAMP POST BOOK

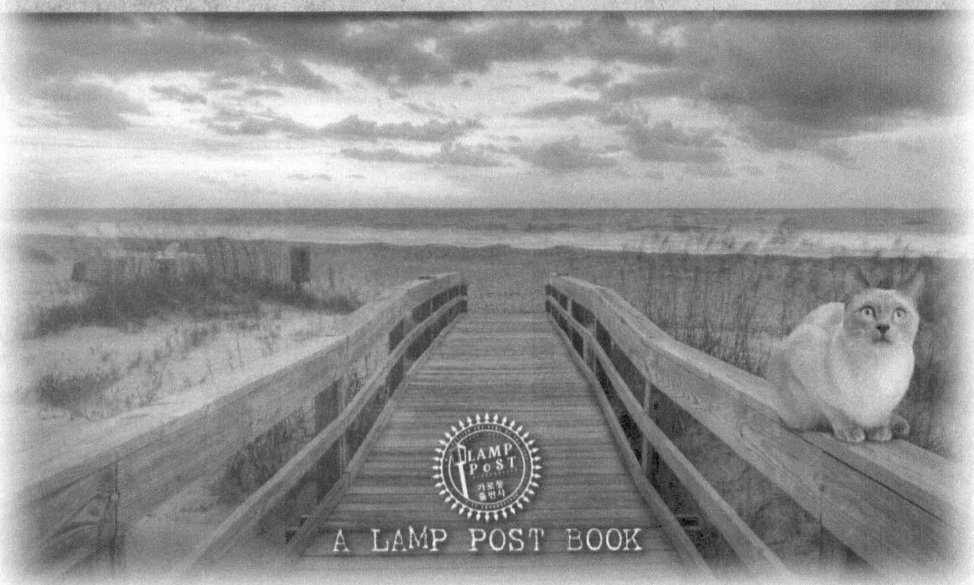

TERROR ON TYBEE ISLAND
BY DEBORAH MALONE

ISBN 10: 1-60039-214-8
ISBN 13: 978-1-60039-214-6
ebook ISBN: 978-1-60039-728-8

www.lamppostpubs.com

TERROR ON TYBEE ISLAND

a Trixie Montgomery cozy mystery

BY DEBORAH MALONE

Look at the birds of the air; they do not sow or reap
or store away in barns, and yet your heavenly Father
feeds them. Are you not much more valuable than they?

Matthew 6:26 (NIV)

ACKNOWLEDGEMENTS

Thank you to all of the readers of the Trixie Montgomery Cozy Mystery series who continue to encourage me to keep writing about Trixie, Dee Dee and Nana. To all the book clubs who have had me as a guest, especially Moulton, Alabama.

A special thank you to Beverly Nault, editor extraordinaire, who keeps the girls out of too much trouble.

Dedication

Terror on Tybee Island is dedicated to my family and friends who continue to encourage me.

A special dedication to Travis Williams – your encouragement and support are the wind beneath my wings.

CHAPTER ONE

O h – My – Goodness! There she is!" Dee Dee tugged on my arm. Dee Dee, who some considered Rubenesque, did not tug gently. I sent up a silent prayer the affronted limb would stay attached. "Who? Where?"

"It's her. Paula Deen." Dee Dee stopped in her tracks and pointed to a stylish woman exiting a limo. "Paula. Yoo Hoo. Over here, Paula." Dee Dee's arm gyrated like a helicopter blade.

Nana hopped up and down. "Paula. I'm your biggest fan!"

Sure, I liked Paula, too. But I didn't plan on making a fool of myself. Okay, I admit I've made a fool of myself several times without planning, but this wouldn't be one of them. Mama must have noticed the panicked look on my face.

"Don't worry sweetie. I'm sure she's used to fans vying for her attention." Mama, the quietest of the bunch, threw up her arm and waved wildly to Paula.

I couldn't believe my eyes – Paula waved back. Then she walked toward us. As she approached, I labored to breathe.

"Hey, y'all," Paula said. "How ya' doin' today? I just love and appreciate all my fans." Dressed in a matching watermelon-colored ensemble, and not one of her stunning white hairs out of place, she was beautiful. "Why don't y'all come and eat with me? I'm having a special taping tomorrow and would love for you to be in the audience. 'Bye now." She wiggled her fingers in a princess wave as she maneuvered through the throng of fans and into her famous restaurant, The Lady and Sons, located in downtown Savannah. A young lady accompanying Paula handed us tickets while instructing us to arrive by two the next afternoon.

"Did you see that, Missy?" Nana's pet name for me, reserved for occasions when she wants to make a point.

"Yes I did, Nana. I'm impressed." I gave her a little squeeze.

"What do you think, Trix?" Dee Dee laid her hand on my shoulder. "How about we come back tomorrow for the taping? This would be great research for your article." Dee Dee was right. Harv, my editor and mentor at *Georgia by the Way*, wanted me to write about Savannah's landmarks as well as her rich history. I made a mental note to research the building that housed Paula's restaurant. Attending a live show could give my story a unique slant.

"Sure. I say let's go for it. Mama, are you in?"

Mama's eyes widened. "Oh, I'd love to attend a live show."

Nana squealed. "I'm going to see Paula. I'm going to see Paula," she trilled.

I went inside and made reservations while the girls window shopped. They hadn't gone far when I returned. We walked up and down the busy sidewalks keeping pace with the other tourists. A bus, the color of a bluebird, with advertisements of tours brightly painted on the sides, drove past. I jotted down the name splashed across the back. We were still oohing and aahing at the sights when Mama noted the time. Reservations awaited us at Seaside Cottage, a bed and breakfast located on the beach.

A wood-carved sign hung by the doorway inviting guests to "Come On In." I stepped into an open, airy room furnished with bright, colorful pieces. I especially admired the hand-tatted doilies and antique seabird collection.

"Hello! Anybody home?"

Red wing-backed chairs scattered around gave the large area

a homey feel. An off-white couch faced a huge rock fireplace with a hand-hewn wooden mantel. Built-in bookshelves filled with sailor pipes flanked each side.

A Tiffany lamp provided light for an antique roll-top desk placed in the corner. It was a cozy little area. Pictures of seascapes and other nature themed paintings adorned the walls. Colorful throw rugs covered the shiny hardwood floors.

Dee Dee, Mama, and Nana were gushing over the motif, when a lady Mama's age decked out in white capris, a bright orange shirt, and the cutest matching flip-flops entered the room. "Hi. Sorry I wasn't here to meet you. I was out back talking to my neighbor."

Mama hesitantly approached her. "Laura?"

"Betty Jo?" They giggled like schoolgirls and ran toward each other with open arms.

"Oh, I'm so excited to see you." After a prolonged hug, Laura stepped back and gave Mama a long look. "You haven't changed a bit since high school."

"Your nose is growing, Laura." They hugged again. "Please let me introduce my sidekicks." Mama turned toward us.

She pulled me close. "This is my daughter, Trixie, and this is her friend, Dee Dee."

While I offered a hand to shake, Dee Dee stepped up and gave Laura a hug like she was her long lost cousin. Bless her heart, that's the kind of person she is. Without a doubt, I'm blessed to have her in my life.

"And I'm Belle, Betty Jo's aunt." Nana didn't wait for introductions. "Please call me Nana, everyone does."

"I'm so pleased all of you could spend your vacation with me." Three Heinz 57 dogs entered the room. Their barking drowned out any further conversation.

"Hush, boys," Laura scolded, but they only barked louder. She raised her voice. "Please excuse me for a minute. I have a friend involved in dog rescue and I volunteered to help while she's sick. Let me put 'em in the outside pen." Laura held out a treat and the dogs tagged along like she was their mama.

The dogs' barking subsided, replaced by angry voices. Several minutes passed and we were beginning to worry when Laura stomped back in, red-faced, nostrils flaring.

"I could just strangle her." She shook her head.

Eyes wide, Mama asked, "Who?"

"That woman next door, Grace Watkins. I could just strangle her. I'm sorry. Since I took in the dogs the old snoot has complained to anybody who'd listen. She's so afraid they're going to dig up her precious turtle eggs." She stopped her tirade. "Oh my goodness, y'all don't want to hear all this. Let me get you settled, then come on down for some refreshments."

As Laura led the way upstairs to our bedrooms, we regarded each other with a deer in the head-light look, wondering what had just happened. My leg was still a little sore from recent knee replacement surgery, so I brought up the rear. Laura showed Mama and Nana their room first. I stuck my head in and eyed a comfy room painted deep coral, accented with a seashell border, and two antique iron sleigh beds. I knew they'd love staying in this gorgeous room.

While they unpacked, Laura showed me and Dee Dee where we'd sleep. Walls the color of the sea greeted us. Dropped shelves around the top of the walls displayed every size and shape of shell imaginable.

The double canopies reminded me of my childhood home. White beds accented with white spreads made the room a little girl's dream come true.

"Oh, Laura, how beautiful!" I turned around to take in the whole room. "Thank you for opening your home to us. Mama's been ecstatic since you invited us to stay."

"I second everything she said." Dee Dee claimed the bed nearest the bathroom. In the past she'd been plagued with frequent nature calls, but when she began to wear one of those new patches, she was able to go a few hours without making a potty stop. But she still automatically parked herself nearest the facilities.

"Okay, ladies. When you get through, come down and help yourselves to the snacks in the dining area." She left us to unpack.

I couldn't wait to freshen up, I felt like a wilted sunflower.

Dee Dee looked out the window. "Wow. What a view, Trix." She held the curtain open and pointed. I could only glimpse a bit of the beach from where I stood across the room. She swiveled back around to soak in more of the panorama. "Oh no!"

"Oh no, what?" I stuck my head next to Dee Dee's, wondering what she'd seen. Down below, Laura, feet apart and hands on hips, was arguing with someone.

CHAPTER TWO

Would you look at that?" Dee Dee motioned toward the women.

"Laura looks like she's about to blow a gasket."

"Yeah, she does. But look at the other woman. I've never seen arms move so fast. She's going to levitate if she doesn't slow those limbs down." Dee Dee imitated the woman's gesturing and bonked me in the arm.

"Ow!" I rubbed the bruised limb. "What do you think they're arguing about?"

"It's a mystery. Remember, she mentioned her neighbor earlier. And not so complimentary.

"I spotted another bed and breakfast, Ocean View Inn, right next door. I imagine the competition promotes some hard feelings."

Dee Dee shoved me over for a better glance. The neighbor lady gazed at our window. Then Laura looked, too. "Quick, duck. They're looking this way." We stumbled more than ducked.

"Maybe Laura will tell us about it later," Dee Dee said. She took an armload of clothes from her suitcase and neatly arranged them in the dresser drawer.

"You're right. There's a chance she'll confide in Mama since they're friends." I claimed a drawer of my own.

"Yoo Hoo. What ya' thinking about, Trixie?" Dee Dee plopped her suitcase on the floor startling me.

"So glad we're friends and you could come with me."

"Well, I feel the same way." Dee Dee walked over and gave me a quick hug. "Isn't this room just the cat's meow?"

Laughter bubbled up my throat and flowed over. I wasn't surprised at Dee Dee's description of our room. Her five cats have the privilege of being treated like her offspring. Since her children, Stephanie and Trey, had moved out of the house she'd projected her motherly love on her fur babies.

"The room is lovely. A great place to rest and rejuvenate. I wish I didn't have to work, but Harv wants me to write on Savannah and Tybee Island while we're here. He promised not to call since I'm on a working vacation." Harv harbored a soft spot in that heart of his, but when it came to his magazine he was serious as a rookie breaking his first big story.

"Come on, let's go see what Mama and Nana are up to." I switched off the lamp and noted the clear base filled with seashells. What a unique idea! Observing the display of shells dispersed around the room, I mentally named this the "seashell room." I couldn't wait to get my feet in the sand and water and hunt for my own shells.

We exited our room the same time as Mama and Nana. Dee Dee grabbed Nana's arm. "Come on, ladies. Let's see what kind of trouble we can get into."

"Bite your tongue, girl." Dee Dee and I'd had our fill of adventures. I didn't want any more for a while.

"Mama, how's your room?"

"Oh, Trixie. I couldn't be more pleased. Thank you again for letting us tag along. I'm so grateful Laura offered us her home."

"Yeah. Did you see the view out your window? The ocean's beautiful. It reminds me of a sparkling jewel."

Dee Dee glanced my way with raised eyebrows. I knew she was remembering the argument between Laura and the unidentified woman.

"Hey there. I see y'all made it back down," our hostess greeted. "How about some crackers and cheese? I try to have snacks in the afternoon and evening. The sea air can sure make a body hungry, and I want my guests to be able to eat whenever they feel the need." Laura had laid out a large spread of snacks. Crackers, cheese, olives, chips, tiny sandwiches, and desserts covered the table.

We grabbed plates and filled them with goodies. I could see it wasn't going to be easy to avoid gaining weight on this vacation. Looking around, I suspected I wouldn't be alone.

I glanced around for other guests. A beautiful, red-headed woman walked in the dining area. A creamy, smooth porcelain complexion and a figure to kill for completed the package.

She sauntered over and extended her hand. "Hi y'all. I'm Ellie Sloan." We shook hands and introduced ourselves. "My, look at this feast. Laura really knows how to take care of her guests."

"Ellie, it's nice to meet you." I was dying to find out what she did for a living. "I write for *Georgia by the Way*, a historic magazine. We're here on vacation, and a little work."

"I'm here for the Save the Turtles Convention. We meet once a year on different coasts to promote protection for the sea turtles' nesting. Did you know that Tybee Island is home to the Loggerhead and Leatherback turtles, as well as the rare Diamondback terrapin? This makes it a great place to have the convention." She flipped back her long red hair.

"Save the turtles? My land, who ever heard of anybody meeting to save turtles? I didn't know they needed any help from people." Nana shook her head.

"Nana. Is it all right to call you that?" She nodded and Ellie continued. "The sea turtles lay their eggs on the beach and then abandon the nest. It takes months for the eggs to hatch and there are so many hazards and predators, including the human kind, that can damage or destroy the eggs."

I'd heard about the sea turtles and their plight, but knew little about the movement to save them.

"Think this would be a good subject for your story, Trixie?" Dee Dee filled her plate with seconds. As Dee Dee loved to eat, I didn't believe it'd be her last.

"Sure. I want to write on a variety of topics."

"I've gathered a lot of material on the sea turtles. You're welcome to read it," Ellie offered.

Laura replenished the table with little pimento cheese and cucumber cream cheese sandwiches. "There's a big initiative on Tybee to protect the turtles. Between May and October, the nesting season, outside lights directed toward the beach must be turned off. The hatchlings will go toward the lights instead of the ocean, and be stranded inland, or worse, run over by cars as they are attracted to the headlights. There's a hefty fine for people who don't adhere to the lighting restrictions."

"Who would have thought?" Mama refilled her plate with sandwiches and chips then settled on an overstuffed loveseat. "Back home we let our turtles fend for themselves."

"Well, you better not say that around here. I'm sure the sea turtles are a worthy cause, but we have some fanatics like my next door neighbor." Laura filled a plate and sat next to Mama. It was good to see Mama's face bright with excitement. She was thrilled when she found out about the trip and getting reacquainted with her friend.

"I for one think it's a great cause." Ellie shook a chip toward Laura making her point. "And I know for a fact that other guests attending the convention will be staying on the island. You have to admit it's good for business."

"I'm sorry, Ellie." Laura looked sheepish as she apologized. "Grace Watkins is about to drive me crazy."

"Why?" Dee Dee was never one to worry about subtlety.

"The dogs. I can't help they got out and started digging up one of the nests. Grace didn't hesitate to report me, and believe me I paid for their little escapade."

"Is that who you were arguing with outside a while ago?" I nudged Dee Dee, but it didn't faze her. She plowed right on. "We looked out the window to admire the ocean view and saw y'all on the beach. You certainly didn't look like you were best friends."

"Yeah, that's her. Grace threatened to report me if the dogs got out again. They told me if I had another citation I'd have to go to court. I'm sure they'd make me give up the dogs. She's an old busy body. There's not a person on this island she hasn't angered at one time or another."

CHAPTER THREE

Iunderstand why she might get under your skin." Dee Dee said around a mouth full.

"Well, I don't want any of this ruining your stay. It's my problem." Laura replenished our drinks and sat back down beside Mama. The doorbell rang.

"Must be more guests." Laura jumped up from the couch and fast footed her way to the front door. "Hello, come on in. Welcome to Seaside Cottage. I'm so glad you've chosen to stay with us."

"We didn't have much choice," a gravelly voice announced. "Most of the hotels were full because of some doggone turtle festival or somesuch nonsense." The red-faced man was as big around as he was tall. He sported a comb-over and a missing tooth. Not exactly Adonis.

Laura, a pained look on her face, led the couple into the sitting room.

"Now, Harold. Be nice." It seemed Harold got the better end of the deal. An attractive, sixty-something lady, decked out in a brightly flowered sundress, patted him on the arm.

She glanced in our direction. "I'm so sorry. Harold's a little on edge, with the long travel and all. I'm Cassie Daniels and this is my husband." She pointed toward the rude man. "We're thrilled to be staying here. I've always wanted to vacation on the beach."

"Humph." Harold surveyed the room with a sneer on his lips.

"We were just having a few snacks and socializing. Why don't you leave your luggage in the foyer and I'll show you to your room later."

Laura introduced us and handed them each a plate. "Please help yourself."

Harold might not have been impressed with his accommodations, but he piled his dish to overflowing.

We relaxed and ate while Laura puttered around. Another knock had Laura scurrying to the door.

A gray-haired, older gentleman stood nobly in the doorway. "Name's George Knight. I just stopped by to introduce myself. I'm a guest at Ocean View Inn." The distinctive English accent suited him well.

Laura tripped over her words. "Please, please come in." She stuck out her hand as did George. The two outstretched hands culminated in a hearty handshake. George appeared to be in his late seventies or early eighties. Dressed in khakis, a dark blue polo, and a tweed jacket thrown over his arm, he posed a dashing figure. Gray hair, blue eyes the color of his shirt, and a wide white smile accentuated his handsomeness.

This did not go unnoticed by Nana, who jumped up to insinuate herself into the conversation.

"Hi, I'm Belle. This is my niece Betty Jo, my great-niece Trixie, and her friend Dee Dee." Her hand shot out and grabbed George's hand faster than a duck on a June Bug. She didn't even mention her nickname. "We're here on vacation."

Dee Dee poked me in the side and stage whispered in my ear, "Nana's got her eye on him."

"Hello, Belle. It's my pleasure to meet you." He held her hand a little longer than necessary. It was good to see Nana flirting with someone her own age. Lately, Nana had taken to making eyes at much younger men.

"Mr. Knight, we were just having a snack. Would you like to stay a while and visit?" Laura thrust a plate and napkin toward George.

"Well," his gaze lingered on Nana, "I do believe I would like that very much." Laura finished the introductions while George filled his plate with goodies. He told us about his travels around the world and his fellow guests at the Ocean View Inn.

He stood to leave.

"Mr. Knight, we're so glad you came by. Please, visit any time."

"Thank you so much, Laura. I sure wish I'd known about this place before I made my reservations."

My ears perked up and I shot a quick glance at Dee Dee.

"Not that I like to talk about anyone, especially my hostess, but that lady could take some lessons from you. She possesses no social skills." He directed his comments to Laura.

A trace of a smile appeared on Laura's face. "Well, Mr. Knight. Please know that you're welcome here anytime."

"Oh, call me George. And I thank you for the invitation. I suppose I've just about worn out my welcome, so I'll be on my way. I enjoyed the snacks and I enjoyed the company even more." He bowed in Nana's direction. Her face turned radish-red.

After George left, our little band dispersed. Nana, Mama, Dee Dee and I opted to take a nap before supper. I awoke to the smell of fried chicken. *Fried chicken*? By the time Dee Dee and I ambled downstairs, we found Mama and Nana settled in the sitting room looking at magazines.

"Is that fried chicken I smell?" Dee Dee raised her nose in the air and sniffed.

"It sure is." Nana scooted over on the loveseat and patted the cushion. I sat down beside her. "Laura's cooking up a good ole southern meal just for us." Nana knows a southern meal when she smells one.

I found it ironic we'd traveled to the best seafood area in the south and we feasted on a meal of fried chicken, mashed potatoes, gravy, green beans and all the trimmings. It would have been rude to go into town on our first night, but I was looking forward to sampling some of the local dishes. We ate until we thought we couldn't eat another bite and then stuffed ourselves on fresh strawberry shortcake. No use in offending our hostess, after all.

Feeling guilty over the calorie laden meal, Dee Dee and I decided to take a walk on the beach. "Oh-my-goodness. If we eat like this all week long, I'm going to gain ten pounds. Or more." Dee Dee patted her rotund stomach.

"You and me both." We laughed at our dilemma.

"Let me grab my camera."

Dee Dee headed outside to wait on me.

On the beach, I gazed at the beautiful landscape God had painted – the dark blue ocean against the soft blue of the sky, surrounded by the white sand. I snapped shot after shot, but a photograph would fall short of capturing this beauty. I reveled in the decision to spend my vacation on Tybee Island. A peace settled over me. If I'd only known what lay in store I wouldn't have felt so peaceful.

"Look!" Dee Dee pointed toward a gray and black cat walking along the edge of the ocean.

"I wonder if he's a stray. Look, his ear's clipped. Means he's had his shots." I'd heard of beach cats, but had never seen one. Roaming the shores, they fed off fish and the food people gave them. Beach cats claimed no permanent home. "He's a little scraggy, but he's a beautiful color." Dee Dee knelt down and called to the kitty.

"Here kitty, kitty." I couldn't believe my eyes. With deliberate steps he cautiously moved toward Dee Dee. "I wish I had something to give him." The cat crouched, looked at her, then slinked a few steps forward. He repeated this until he was within inches of her. When she reached out to pet him he darted away.

I picked up a shell and studied the patterns of gray, brown, and white, similar to the cat's coloring. God's hand was everywhere. *Father, thank you for giving us this beautiful world to live in. Help me to take the time to stop and enjoy it.*

"Come on, Trix. Let's go back in." Dee Dee interrupted my thoughts. "It's been a long day and we need to rest up for some sightseeing." She grabbed my arm and we walked back to Laura's arm and arm. *Thank you, God, for my best friend.*

Later that evening, we sat around with Ellie, Cassie, Harold, and Laura. Everyone chatted about their day and plans for the week. Dusk arrived and our group broke up. Ellie went out on the town and the Daniels left for a nighttime drive. We decided to turn in for the night, and get an early start in the morning.

I didn't know if it was excitement or if I'd gone to bed too early, but I couldn't sleep. I tossed and turned most of the night. I threw back the covers and grabbed the clock. When the bright red numerals glared four o'clock, I knew it was useless to stay in bed. I thought a walk on the beach might relax me, so I quietly donned my capris and a t-shirt and stealthily snuck down the stairs.

I grabbed a flashlight that sat by the door. Outside, the brightness of a full moon greeted me. The rounded orb appeared so close I wanted to reach out and touch it. The moon's reflection on the ocean shone like sparkling jewels.

"Meow. Meow." It was the beach cat. When we had come in from our walk, Laura told us the locals had named him Captain Jack. He was digging at something in the sand. I tiptoed closer expecting him to run. He didn't right away, but when I encroached on his territory he fled. My flashlight beam reflected on something shiny dangling from his mouth as he escaped.

I directed the light back to where he'd been digging. I noticed a big lump in the sand. Had someone thrown a pile of trash on the beach? Boy, were they in for a hefty fine if caught.

I walked closer and shined the light to get a better look. Then I realized it wasn't trash. It wasn't seaweed and it wasn't driftwood. These wouldn't be covered in blood. A body with a smashed in head would.

My body shook and I wanted to run, but my legs wouldn't move. A morbid curiosity drew my eyes to the ghoulish sight. The peaceful sounds of the ocean were shattered by a scream. Mine.

CHAPTER FOUR

After I discovered the body identified as that of a Mrs. Grace Watkins, several officers arrived to investigate the crime scene. They instructed us to gather in Laura's house, including everyone from Ocean View Inn.

Sipping from my steaming mug in Laura's living room, I surveyed the eclectic group of guests. Ellie and the Daniels sat across from me. Mama, Nana, and Dee Dee were on the edge of their seats, ready to rescue me if I fainted. George and Laura, both expressionless, occupied the wingback chairs. In my fugue state I recognized these people, but there were several unfamiliar faces.

"Hey, y'all. Ain't this the most fascinating thing you've ever seen? I just love to watch those murder mysteries on the Investigation Discovery Channel." A guest from Ocean View Inn introduced himself as Bubba Maxwell. This man definitely lived up to his name.

"Mr. Maxwell, this is not a television show. This is real, and someone lost their life. I'd appreciate it if you showed a little respect." I had a feeling this was a concept lost on Bubba, but Detective Joe Baker was giving him the benefit of the doubt.

George and Bubba weren't the only guests from Grace's bed and breakfast. It seems she had collected a menagerie of folks. A couple of young newlyweds, covered in tattoos and pierced with rings in every orifice that showed, and probably some that didn't, sat slumped on a couch. At first glance I wasn't sure I'd want to encounter them in the dark.

A man dressed in an expensive business suit, sporting a pair of faux-croc oxfords, spoke to the group, "Hi, I'm John Porter." He didn't elaborate on his introduction.

Wow, he sure looks sharp as a tack. I wonder what he's doing on Tybee.

The detective's baritone voice interrupted my thoughts. "Some of you will be interviewed separately by either Officer Judy Caldwell or Officer Ben Stevens." Detective Baker peered at each person through squinted eyes. "The rest of you will be lucky enough to be interviewed by me."

I chanced a long look at the detective. Tall, broad shouldered and a little on the hefty side, he exuded authority. I wondered if he'd grown up on the island. His skin was tanned and weather-worn. He had a head full of dark hair tinged with gray and possessed expressive brown eyes. He sported a thick mustache. He reminded me of Tom Selleck in Magnum P.I., albeit a bit heavier.

"Well, Detective. You're lucky my Trixie found the body." Nana flashed him a big smile.

"Oh, why is that?" He shot Nana a look that would have unnerved anyone else. Not Nana.

"Let me tell you." I knew Nana had every intention of telling him why. "Trixie, Dee Dee and I have already helped solve two murders. We'll be an asset to your investigation."

The Detective's jaw dropped like a windless kite on the beach. *Way to go Nana. Foot in mouth again.* It was true we'd helped on a couple of other cases, but not because our skills were sought after. It was a matter of saving someone we loved from the slammer. Dee Dee unfortunately became the main suspect of a murder in Dahlonega. That was almost two years ago now. I was grateful we'd been able to find the real killer and keep her from a life behind bars. She'd hate those orange jumpsuits.

A year ago, a friend of Harv's was accused of killing one of his employees. Doc Pennington, the director of the Marietta History Museum, had asked for our help in clearing his name. I tried to stay out of the investigation, but Doc pleaded with us and I caved.

But we weren't asked to help by law enforcement. Just the opposite. We'd been warned to keep our noses out of police business. But I couldn't stand by and let my best friend go to jail for a crime she didn't do. Then when Doc begged us to help him, we melted like butter.

I looked at Detective Baker and he looked right back at me – a stand-off. I blinked first. "Ms. Montgomery."

"Yes." The lump in my throat felt like an orange.

"I don't care how many investigations you *helped* with. You will not be interfering with this one. Is that understood?" He stood with legs parted and hands on his hips. "You'll have me to reckon with me if you interfere.

"Yes sir." I fully intended to heed his warning.

"After all, you found the body. I plan on keeping a close eye on you." I'm sure he would. If it weren't for my Beau, I might not mind if he kept an eye on me. But Beau had asked me to marry him before we left for vacation and I told him I needed this time to make my decision.

I caught a glimpse of Dee Dee. I guess she'd noticed, too, because she was looking at Detective Baker like she could eat him up. What was going on with my friends? First, Nana – smitten with George. Now, Dee Dee was star struck with the investigator.

"Since we're on the subject, I think I'll interview you first, Ms. Montgomery. Officer Caldwell and Officer Stevens, you can start your interviews." He looked around at everyone as he spoke. "No one leaves this house until one of us releases you." The detective looked at Laura. "Ms. Walker, do you have some rooms we can use for questioning?"

"Sure. Follow me." She led us to a room I assumed was her office. A big oak desk was positioned with a lovely view of the ocean. Filing cabinets sat in the corner. Shelves stuffed full of books lined one side of a wall. A floor lamp stood sentinel by a recliner on a beautiful, multi-colored, patchwork brocade rug that covered the hardwood floors.

I chose a maroon rocker-recliner. When I sat down my body oozed into the cushion. I hadn't realized how exhausted I was until now. Detective Baker settled in the office chair and rolled directly in front of me. He leaned forward, hands on knees, close enough for me to smell his English Leather aftershave.

After gazing into my soul, he pulled out his pad, flipped the pages, and poised his pen. "Start from the beginning... may I call you Trixie?"

"Sure." Who was I to argue at this point?

"Okay, Trixie. Tell me why you were on the beach at four in the morning." He flicked the pen back and forth on his pad. It unnerved me.

"I couldn't sleep. After tossing and turning most of the night I decided to take a walk. You know how it's hard to sleep the first night in a new bed." I blushed, but the detective didn't seem to notice. "We ate late, and I had a full tummy."

Without comment, he wrote in his little book. I wondered what he jotted down since I hadn't said much of anything relevant to somebody getting killed. "Go on."

"There's really not much to tell. I'd walked a short way when I spotted Captain Jack, he's the resident beach cat, digging around something. I thought he might be digging up a turtle's nest so I went to investigate. The closer I got, I realized it was something large lying on the beach."

A shiver ran through me as I recalled the discovery. "Then, I thought it was just some garbage, but when the beam from the flashlight hit it I knew it...wasn't." The sight of the bloody body would be seared into my mind forever.

"Did you recognize the person?" He wrote furiously.

"Yes, but..." I wanted to reassure him I hardly knew the woman. "I just arrived today. Yesterday. She was a virtual stranger to me."

"What did you do when you found the body?"

"I screamed, of course," I stated.

"Detective Baker?" He stopped writing and looked straight at me. I had his full attention. "People talk. I've heard Grace didn't have many friends. Instead of acquiring friends she had a talent for making enemies. Don't you think there'd be a long list of suspects who had a motive for murder?" I was as bad as Nana. I couldn't keep my nose out of where it didn't belong.

"Ms. Montgomery. I don't remember saying this was a murder, but I guess it was kind of obvious with the injury she sustained."

Great deduction, Sherlock.

He leaned forward, inches from my face. I could see flecks of gold in his brown eyes. "I don't care how many cases you've helped solve," he didn't need to sound so sarcastic. "You'd better not interfere in my murder investigation." I guess he didn't believe me.

But I knew I was at the top of the suspect list since I'd found the body. Was it interference if I was trying to clear my own name?

CHAPTER FIVE

I longed to talk with Dee Dee to debrief, but Detective Baker called her name as soon as he told me I could go. She jumped up, grinning from ear to ear. She seemed way too eager to be questioned in a murder case. She'd changed clothes and now wore a hot pink pant suit with sandals to match. How she had time to change and put on make-up was a mystery to me. A modern day Houdini?

She followed Detective Baker like a lost little puppy dog. Nana appeared beside me.

"Did you notice Dee Dee's expression?"

"Yes, I did. What do you make of it?"

"Looks like she's taken a liking to the detective," Nana said.

"How about you, Nana? You seem to have your eye on George and I must say he is pleasant to look at."

Nana turned beet red. "What if I do? He's handsome and a gentleman. Not a bad combination in my book. He's been around the world you know."

I gave her a quick shoulder hug. "Aw, Nana. I'm just teasing you. I'm glad you've found a new friend. Maybe you'll get to know each other better while we're here." I had no idea what this week held in store for us. I never in my wildest dreams thought we'd stumble upon another dead body.

"Come on, let's see what Mama's up to." We perched on the couch next to her. I scooted closer.

"Trixie, I'm so sorry you found Grace. It must have been awful." Mama reached over and took my hand in hers. She gave it a squeeze.

"I'll never forget her lifeless body lying in the sand." I shivered at the thought. "It doesn't matter how much you're disliked, no one deserves to die in that manner."

"Of course not. But according to Laura, she made enemies like a dog draws fleas. Detective Baker has his work cut out for him."

We chatted for a while then sat in silence until Dee Dee returned. Detective Baker asked if we knew where Laura was. I guessed she was next in line for questioning.

Mama pointed towards the kitchen. "She's in there, Detective."

Dee Dee made a bee-line to the table filled with sweets. "Wow, look at this. Laura sure knows how to take care of her guests." Frayed nerves must have plagued her but they didn't seem to interfere with her appetite because she filled her plate with goodies. "Scoot over." She plopped down, squeezing in-between Nana and me.

"How did the questioning go?"

"That Detective Baker is something else. He was so thorough in his interrogation. I wish I'd had more to tell him." She took a big bite of a cream-filled donut. The cream oozed out the other end. She took a minute to chew then proclaimed, "I have no doubt he'll have this case solved in no time at all."

I was right. She was smitten.

We talked for a while, and then roamed around the inn. Several hours passed before all of the guests had been questioned. At the detective's request everyone gathered in the living room.

Detective Baker stood tall, reaching his fullest height. He hiked up his pants and placed his hand on the gun strapped in his shoulder holster. "We've interviewed every person from the Seaside Cottage and Ocean View Inn for now. You are free to roam the Island, but please stay within the area in case you're needed. We'll ask some of you to come down to the department for further questioning."

"How about Savannah, Detective? Can we visit there?" George moved from behind Bubba.

"Savannah's fine. Just leave your information with Officer Caldwell or Officer Stevens if you haven't already."

He tipped his head in our direction, but his gaze lingered on Dee Dee. "Ladies, I'll talk to you later." With that, he was on his way. Dee Dee swooned to my side of the couch.

"Dee Dee, get a grip."

Laura addressed the guests of the Ocean View Inn. "This is a terrible thing to happen while you're staying at Grace's house. I want you to know you're welcome to come over any time to socialize or share a meal. I'm inviting all of you to the Seaside Cottage for dinner tonight. I'll be serving at seven."

"That's right nice of you. I'll be sure and be here around then," Bubba said.

"Yes. That is more than kind. I would like to come, too." George shot Nana a glance.

"Okay. That settles it. I'll see you for dinner." After Laura completed her announcement, the guests went their separate ways. That left Nana, Mama, Dee Dee, and me alone with Laura.

"Ladies, if you don't mind I'm going to take a nap. I'm wiped out and I have a lot to do to get dinner ready." Laura's voice shook. "I'm so sorry this happened on your vacation. Grace might have been a thorn in my side, but I'd never wish this on her. It's scary to think the killer is still on the loose and in the neighborhood." She chewed on a fingernail.

Mama placed her arm around Laura's shoulder. "Don't worry about a thing. I'm glad we're here so we can support you during this awful time. Go lay down and we'll see you this evening." Laura let Mama guide her toward her room.

"You heard the Detective. He said we could go to Savannah. If we hurry we'll have time to clean up, change clothes, and head on over to Paula's. After all, she did ask me to come." Nana put her hands on her hips daring anyone to deny she was Paula's new best friend.

"I don't know, Nana. So much has happened. Maybe we should stick around here for a while." I wanted to go to Paula's as much as the next person, but finding the body had put a damper on my spirits. I didn't feel like doing much of anything and I hadn't slept all night.

"Come on, Trix." Dee Dee pulled out her pitiful face from her bag of tricks. "I know you've been through a lot, but a trip to watch the taping will help lighten the mood." She put her arm around my shoulder, pulled me close, and gave me a big squeeze. "Aw, come on."

I didn't have a chance with Nana and Dee Dee in cahoots. "Let's ask Mama if she feels like going. She might be too tired to go."

"What? Too tired to go and watch the special cooking show she's taping in her restaurant? This is a chance in a million. I wouldn't miss it for anything." Obviously, Mama wasn't as tired as I thought she was.

Nana and Dee Dee did a little happy dance while Mama grinned from ear to ear. I was definitely outnumbered. Maybe it would do me good to get away for a while.

Dee Dee drove while I dozed, and we made it to downtown Savannah, one of the most beautiful cities in the South. Moss-draped trees lined the streets. Historic homes and buildings comprised most of the downtown area. Yawning and stretching, I looked out the window at the gracious buildings full of history.

I'd researched Savannah so I'd have ample background material for my article. Founded in 1733, it became the first city in Georgia. Originally laid out in four squares, each consisting of eight city blocks, by 1851 it had grown to 24 squares with 22 squares left today.

Dee Dee whipped my little PT Cruiser into a handicapped parking space.

I'd recently splurged on a new car. I'd traded in my beloved Jeep because I needed dependable transportation for my job. Actually, my Cruiser wasn't brand new, but it was new to me. A few thousand miles logged onto the odometer made it an affordable buy. I loved the light cream color and for a bonus it came with a convertible top.

This past year I was the recipient of a new knee, thanks to a knee replacement. Even though the result had been nothing less than remarkable, I still had to be careful. If I walked too much, my knee ached. I rarely needed a cane anymore, but it was helpful to park as close as I could to my destination.

The Lady and Sons, located at the corner of Whitaker and Congress streets, was a favorite place for tourists. By the time we arrived, a line snaked down the sidewalk. Thank goodness we had tickets.

I'd brought my camera, a necessity in my line of work. I clicked pictures of the crowd as they stood around waiting for their turn to enter. I took several shots of historic buildings while we waited.

We stood with other anxious tourists when a black limo pulled up to the entrance. Out stepped Paula. The crowd went wild, cheering and pushing to get a glimpse of her.

"Paula, Paula!" Nana pushed her way through the throng until she found an opening. She threw up her arm and waved vigorously. "Did you see that? She waved to me." I wasn't about to pop Nana's balloon. If she believed Paula waved to her then who was I to disagree?

Once the line started moving it wasn't long before we were settled in our seats. The dining area was large and open. Ivy covered wallpaper adorned the walls. Oak wood tables covered with white tablecloths filled the room. On each table was a vase filled with multi-colored, fresh flowers. There wasn't an empty seat in the place.

While the guests were served, a young woman stepped up to the front of the room and explained the filming process. We were instructed when to clap, and reminded to wait for permission to get out of our seats. I glanced at Dee Dee, glad she was wearing a fresh patch and wouldn't have any emergencies, or she might miss the taping altogether. In a few minutes, quiet filled the room as Paula made her entrance.

Bouncing out, she was dressed in a pretty lavender pant suit and her beautiful smile welcomed us.

"Hey y'all!"

The audience answered with a warm hello and applause. She went right into cooking the selected meal. We were served the same menu: salad, fried green tomatoes, baked chicken, macaroni and cheese, collard greens, and a choice of banana pudding or peach cobbler for desert.

My mouth watered in anticipation. We dug in while Paula asked who her number one fan was. Most people raised their hands – not Nana. She stood up and made her way toward the front. A young woman with a clipboard rushed to stop her, but Paula waved her off.

"Hey there! And what's your name?" Paula guided Nana over just a bit so she didn't block the camera's view.

"Belle. It's so good to be here. I just love your show. There's something I've been wanting to ask you. How do you get your hair to stay in place all the time?" *Way to go Nana.*

I thought I saw Paula roll her eyes, but like a trooper she laughed and moved right along. She even let Nana help with some of the recipes. Everything moved smoothly until she made the fatal mistake.

"Belle, I'd like you to taste some of the goodies we've made." She forked up a big bite of collard greens. "Here, try some of these. I just know you're gonna' love 'em. It's my dear mama's recipe."

Nana took the fork and slowly put it into her mouth. Then she took a minute and savored the taste. Everyone held their breath waiting her approval.

"mmm. Delicious."

Paula heaved a sigh of relief. Only to be blindsided by Nana. "But, I think they could use a tad more sugar. It would help smooth out that bitter taste." She leaned over to whisper in Paula's ear unaware the microphone picked up her every word. "You can add a little beer, too. My family hasn't figured out my secret ingredient yet."

That's why they taste so good? Beer? Oh my goodness. Mama's eyes were about to pop out of her head, Dee Dee stood up and waved to Nana, and I wanted to duck under the table. Especially when I noticed all eyes turned our way.

Paula couldn't guide Nana off the stage fast enough. "Thank you, Belle, for your help." She motioned to someone to get Nana back to her seat.

Nana wore a grin from ear to ear as she sat down at our table. "Well, it's not every day you get to be a taste tester for Paula Deen. Aren't you glad I talked you into coming, Trixie?" *God, please forgive me for the thoughts invading my head right now. I don't really want to kill Nana.*

It was all I could do to get through the meal even though it was some of the best Southern fare I'd ever eaten. As soon as we finished we high tailed it out of there. I don't think it was soon enough for us. Or Paula.

"Nana, what were you thinking when you told Paula she needed more sugar in her collards? And you've been putting beer in yours all these years?" Mama's voice was unnaturally high pitched.

"I was being truthful. She asked me what I thought."

"No, Nana. She asked you how they tasted. I don't think she really wanted your opinion on her recipe."

"It sure was a memorable day. Right girls?" Leave it to Dee Dee to find the good in a situation. She'd been my rock more times than I could remember. When Wade left me, my life as I knew it had fallen apart. Not only had I lost my husband, I lost my house too. Unknown to me, Wade had made financial decisions that left us in ruins.

Mama, bless her heart, had urged me to return to Vans Valley and stay in her garage apartment while I sorted out my future. When I moved back, I was lower than a snake's belly. Dee Dee took me under her wing and supported me during a rough time. She's been there for me ever since. *Thank you, God, for my friend.*

After we returned to Laura's we had enough time for a quick nap. The good Lord knew I needed it. I sank down on the feather soft bed and felt like I was floating on a cloud. I was asleep as soon as my head hit the pillow. Next thing I knew I was dreaming that Paula Deen was screaming at Nana for ruining her show. The crowd at the restaurant stood, turned our way, and chanted, "Throw them out. Throw them out."

An angry customer shook me by the shoulders. "Trixie! Trixie!" How did she know my name? I managed to pry open my eyes, struggling to awaken from this awful nightmare. I was surprised to discover a goofy looking face inches from mine. I yelped, and Dee Dee jumped back.

"What are you doing? You scared the starch out of me." I sat up in bed and tried to clear the images of an angry Paula from my head.

"I was trying to wake you. I can't help it if you were dead to the world." Dee Dee sat on the other bed. "I called and called, but you kept right on snoring."

"Sure I did. I don't snore."

Dee Dee laughed so hard I thought she was going to fall back on the bed. "Come on and get up. Your mama stopped by and said dinner was about ready to be served."

"It can't be that late." I looked at the bedside clock to see for myself. Sure enough it was almost seven.

"Yep. We slept longer than I thought we would, but the trip took a lot out of us. Go ahead and I'll wait on you to get ready," Dee Dee said.

A few minutes later we walked down to the dining room together. A crowd had already gathered. It looked like everybody from the Ocean View Inn was in attendance: George Knight, Bubba Maxwell, Kiki and Nick Sanderson, and John Porter.

George sat by Nana and Mama sat next to her. Ellie sat next to Cassie and her husband Harold sat next to her. There were two empty chairs for Dee Dee and me at a table occupied by Bubba and John.

"Ladies, take a seat," Laura waved across our table. "Louise, my fabulous cook, is going to help me serve." She returned to the kitchen. When Laura and Louise walked back into the dining room their arms were laden with food. Fresh fish was the entrée for the evening. Side dishes included slaw, hush puppies, green beans, and baked potatoes. Now this is what I'd been waiting for with baited breath: a fresh seafood meal.

Talk around the tables focused on Grace's death.

Who would do something like this? Why would someone do this? And the burning question was, "Is the killer or killers still in the neighborhood?"

Laura urged all of us to retire to the living room for coffee and our choice of bread pudding, or chocolate cake. That's where we were when the doorbell rang. Louise promptly answered the door.

"Ms. Laura, there's a man here to see you," she called.

Detective Joe Baker followed her in. "Good evening, people. I'm sorry to interrupt your evening, but I'm here on business." He looked around taking in the crew of guests in attendance. His gaze stayed a little longer on Dee Dee. She smiled like a cat that just finished a bowl of milk, and though he didn't smile back, his eyes said it all with their twinkle.

"Hi, Detective. Were you looking for me?" Laura came in from the kitchen wiping her hands on her apron.

"Yes, ma'am. I need to talk with you. Let's go somewhere private."

We busied ourselves stacking the empty dessert dishes, wondering what the conversation was in the other room. We didn't have long to wait because they returned quicker than a hound dog chasing a coon. Tears trailed down Laura's face. When she spotted Mama she openly cried.

"Oh, Betty Jo. They're taking me in for questioning. The detective said he has evidence that makes me a person of interest. Please, help me."

CHAPTER SEVEN

Don't worry, Laura. I'll wait up until the detective brings you back." Mama gave him a scornful look, daring him to do otherwise.

"I should have her back in a couple of hours." His gaze raked over every person present. "I may have to interview each of you again, so be expecting it."

Mama gave Laura a big hug and with that they were gone.

Everyone talked at once. "Why did they take Laura? When are they going to return with her? Do they suspect her?" We exhausted ourselves with the possibilities until we were out of ideas, and I noticed most of the guests from Ocean View Inn had left except for George. He scooted a little closer to Nana.

"Girls, why don't you go on to bed and I'll wait up for Laura?" Mama stood up and gathered the dessert dishes.

"Watch it Betty Jo," Dee Dee pulled her almost empty dish out of Mama's reach, "I still have another bite." She wasn't about to let go of her second helping of bread pudding.

"I don't know if I can sleep, but I'm sure willing to try." I handed Mama my bowl. "Why don't you let us know when Laura gets back?" I stood up and stretched like a cat waking from a nap.

"Nana, want to come up with us?"

Nana patted George's arm. "I think I'll stay here for a little while longer." She smiled at George and he mirrored her smile.

"Come on, Dee. It looks like it's time for us to hit the hay." I grabbed her arm and pulled her toward the steps.

"You might hit the hay, but I'm going to hit the bed." Dee Dee guffawed.

We retreated to our lovely room. My knee ached, so I soaked in a tub of warm water, hoping to ease the pain. We shared a bathroom with Mama and Nana, but since they decided to stay downstairs a while longer I didn't feel guilty hogging the bathroom.

"I'll just be a few minutes Dee, then you can soak." I surveyed the room while I relaxed. The cozy room boasted white walls with white and black tile floor covering. A border complimenting the color scheme decorated the walls. A unique hand-painted piece of glass hung on the wall. A closer looked illuminated the artist's name, Nancy Smith. I'd heard Seaside Sisters, a variety store located downtown Tybee, sold these special paintings. The Seaside Sisters was definitely on my list of places to visit.

"Hey, have you drowned in there?" Dee Dee hollered from the bedroom.

"Hold on! I'm coming. I'm soaking these old bones."

"Just kidding. Take your time."

A few minutes later I exited the bathroom feeling like a renewed woman.

"Let me see your hands." Dee Dee grabbed my hands and turned them palms up. "Just wanted to see if they look like prunes."

"Ha, ha. Very funny. I'd wager you'll stay as long as I did when you sink down in that claw-foot tub." I sat on my bed and a huge yawn escaped.

"All right, sleepyhead. Go ahead and turn out the lights. I'll be out in a few minutes.

I snuggled under the covers. My relaxed body melded into the soft bed sheets. It was a little bit of heaven on earth. I really wanted to stay up and ask Mama how Laura's interview went. But a few minutes after my head hit the pillow I was sound asleep.

A knock on the bedroom door startled me from deep slumber. "Trixie, you awake?" Mama opened the door just enough to stick her head in.

I sat up in bed and pulled the covers up for warmth. Dee Dee propped up on her elbow to see what was going on. "Sure, Mama. Come on in." The morning sun poured through the window, illuminating the room.

I scrunched my feet up so she could sit on the end of my bed. Mama wore a wrinkled brow and looked like she hadn't slept much.

"Mama, what's the matter?"

"It's Laura. I waited for Detective Baker to bring her back." Mama picked at a loose thread on the cover. "It's not good news."

"What do you mean, Betty Jo?" Dee Dee sat up and swung her feet over the side of the bed.

"They found the murder weapon not far from the body. Laura's fingerprints were all over it."

"What!" My mind couldn't conjure up an image of this sweet lady as a murderer. Then again I suppose anyone pushed to the brink could act on impulse. "What was the murder weapon?"

"A garden gnome."

Dee Dee laughed out loud and I couldn't help but smile. Mama wasn't amused.

"I'm sorry," Dee Dee said through another burst of giggles. "I know it's not funny, but a garden gnome. How could you kill somebody with a garden gnome?"

I took Mama's hand in mine. "Mama, why do they think Laura killed Grace Watkins?"

"I know it seems far-fetched anyone would use a gnome as a murder weapon, but Detective Baker said her head was smashed in by blunt force. The gnome belonged to Laura. She had it in her yard for decoration. You know how popular they've become lately."

"They do seem to be the rave right now. But there must be a hundred gnomes on the island." Dee Dee plunged her feet into her fuzzy cat slippers.

"That's just it. The gnome they found near the body came from Laura's garden, and was custom painted to match the cottage trim. It didn't help it's common knowledge she maintained an on-going feud with Grace." Mama got up and strolled around the room. "She's inconsolable."

"I'm so sorry, Mama." A shiver ran through my body. I grabbed my robe and slid it on.

"Trixie, I have something to confess. Please don't be mad." I couldn't for the life of me think of what she could have done to make me angry.

Mama's my rock. After my divorce, she not only offered me a place to live, but a shoulder to cry on. I owed Mama, even though I knew she didn't feel that way.

"Don't worry, Mama. I'm sure it'll be all right." I put my arm around her.

She sniffed a little and a lone tear rolled down her cheek. "I didn't know what else to do. She was crying and it just popped out of my mouth."

I wondered out loud what had popped out of her mouth. "What are you talking about? I don't understand."

"I told Laura that you'd solved a couple of murders and that you'd help her." She looked over my shoulder. "And I told her Dee Dee would help, too."

"What? You did what, Mama?" Oh my goodness. I wasn't mad, but I sure wasn't doing a happy dance. "I promised I'd keep my distance."

"Wow," Dee Dee managed to squeak out.

I didn't think anything could make Dee Dee speechless. This came close to it.

The bedroom door swung open a tad then flung open the rest of the way. Nana stepped in. "Did you ask them yet?" She looked around the room. "I guess you did. Isn't it great, Trixie? Another murder for us to solve."

CHAPTER EIGHT

Nana, there is no 'we.'" I studied Mama and saw hope shining in her eyes. I hated to disappoint her, but I didn't think it was a good idea to interfere in Detective Baker's investigation. It's true, Dee Dee and I had been instrumental in solving a couple of murders, but I didn't want to make a habit of solving crimes. The local authorities had already made it clear they did not welcome any intrusion.

"Mama, I don't believe we're qualified to help Laura. She needs a professional."

"Laura deserves someone who isn't biased and believes in her. She's a newcomer on the island and with her carefree attitude toward the turtles it'll be hard for her to get a fair shake."

I couldn't say no to the lady who had given so freely when I needed her. I took the chicken's way out. "I'll consider it."

Mama's eyes lit up. "Thank you, Trixie." She gave me a huge squeeze.

I glanced over her shoulder and noticed Dee Dee shaking her head with a big grin plastered on her face. She knew I'd cave.

"This is great. Trixie, you know I'll help you any way possible," Nana said. "Remember, you and Dee Dee probably wouldn't be here if it weren't for me saving your necks in Marietta." She glanced upward. "Well, I did have a little help from the Lord."

As much as I hated to admit it, Nana was right. Less than a year ago, Dee Dee and I had gotten ourselves in a heap of trouble. Three crazy guys kidnapped us and held us at gunpoint. "You got me there, Nana. Come on. Let's go down and discover what's for breakfast."

"Maybe you'd like to put on some clothes first." Dee Dee rolled her eyes heavenward.

I looked at my pajamas. "Oh, I guess you're right. Mama, you and Nana go ahead and we'll be down in a few minutes." Mama left with a smile on her face and a hope she didn't have when she entered.

"Trix, how are you going to help Laura?" Dee Dee donned a bright orange, long-sleeve, pullover shirt. I wondered what color pants she'd wear. Dee Dee's taste for bright clothes matched her personality: upbeat and cheerful.

"I don't know. My gut says I shouldn't get involved lest I risk getting in trouble with Detective Dreamy, but my heart wants to help Laura. Mama's helped me so much. I don't want to disappoint her. Let's go down and talk to Laura after breakfast."

We finished dressing. Dee Dee paired up her shirt with light green pants. It wasn't something I'd wear, but it looked good on her and it was appropriate for the month of October. I had on my usual khaki pants with a light blue pullover. I often envied Dee Dee's ability to dress so brightly, but I couldn't bring myself to break away from my habit of wearing browns and beiges.

By the time we entered the dining room, guests from Seaside Cottage and Ocean View Inn already surrounded the tables. Breakfast consisted of eggs, bacon, sausage, hash browns, grits, waffles, and various pastries. Louise made sure our table remained full of breakfast goodies.

I noticed Laura's absence right away. The talk at our table focused on Grace Watkins' murder. The scuttlebutt was that Grace's niece planned to move to Ocean View Inn. Her long time cook and assistant would keep it open and running until then. The guests at the inn had an open invitation for meals at Seaside Cottage.

I couldn't help but survey the room and wonder if the murderer sat among us. I didn't know these people. What, if any, motive would they possess to murder Grace? Surely her service wasn't that bad. I silently laughed. *Okay Trixie, get a grip.*

"Hey girl, where did you go? I asked you if you were going to eat that sausage sitting on your plate." Dee Dee's fork was poised to jab the lone piece of sausage.

Normally I wouldn't mind, but I felt the need for all the greasy food I could consume. "Sorry, I'm gonna eat it." Her brown, puppy-dog eyes and protruding lip made me acquiesce. "All right, I'll half it with you."

By the time we finished eating, the other guests had left. Nana and Mama walked over and sat at our table. "Trixie, would you talk with Laura now? She's in her room and won't come out. She's in a terrible state."

"Sure, Mama."

I eyed Dee Dee. "You coming?"

"I'm right behind you. I wouldn't miss this for anything." Dee Dee wiped her plate clean with a piece of biscuit. I guess I wasn't the only one who craved cholesterol laden food.

"Trixie, I know you'd like for me to come, too. Being that I'm experienced in these matters. But George has asked me to go sightseeing with him." Nana's grin reminded me of a cat with a feather hanging from its mouth.

"That's all right, Nana. We'll keep you posted." I looked heavenward. *Thank you, Lord, for small favors.*

"Laura?"

She looked up as I stuck my head in the door.

"Can we come in?"

"Okay."

Laura's room was as pretty as the rest of the house. Painted bright blue and accented with white furniture trimmed in gold, it reminded me of the ocean. Laura sat on a canopy bed situated in the middle of the room. She looked lower than an ant on stilts.

Dee Dee walked over and put her arm around Laura's shoulder. I wasn't surprised. When I had gone through my divorce with Wade I had nose-dived to the lowest I'd ever been in my life. I wondered if I'd ever feel human again. Dee Dee took me under her wing and supported me through some hard times and we'd been fast friends since. Dee Dee was a natural-born care giver.

With this simple gesture of empathy, Laura started crying. "What am I going to do? Detective Baker says I'm a person of interest. I know what that means – it means suspect."

Dee Dee glanced at me with a look that shouted "help!"

I shrugged my shoulders, but took a stab at consoling Laura. "Didn't the detective say he was going to interview all the guests? Maybe it was just routine questioning."

"No." Laura sniffed. Dee Dee grabbed a wad of tissues from the bed-side table and handed them to her. "He said my fingerprints are all over the gnome and he knows it came from my garden. Grace and I have had an ongoing squabble since I opened. She accused me of purposely tak-ing away her business." Laura blew her nose and continued.

"I didn't steal her guests. She ran them off with her horrible person-ality. She was a female Attila the Hun. I've never seen anyone so grouchy or vindictive in my life. Her long time guests have now started reserving with me. I don't see how Edna put up with it all these years." Laura rifled through the wadded up tissues for a clean one and dabbed her eyes.

Dee Dee and I spoke in unison. "Who's Edna?"

"Edna is Grace's cook and housekeeper. *Was* her housekeeper, I should say. She treated that woman like dirt, but Edna stayed with her anyway. I always wondered if she had something on Edna to keep her there all these years."

Dee Dee and I shared a knowing look. Did this woman have a motive for murder?

CHAPTER NINE

A frantic knock on Laura's bedroom door demanded our attention.

"Come in," Laura said.

"Come quick, Ms. Laura. The dogs escaped." Louise wrung her hands. "I'm so sorry. I opened the back door to let the dogs out for a little while. They flew out and the gate to the pen was open." Her chin quivered.

"Oh no! Ladies please help me round up the escapees. I've already been fined once. Those blasted sea turtles have caused me nothing but trouble."

We followed Laura downstairs, through the kitchen and outside. I spotted the dogs on the beach, bottoms up, digging for all they were worth. I hoped we'd go unnoticed while they dug.

The dogs stayed so intense on retrieving their prey the mischievous pups didn't have a clue when we snuck up behind them. We carried them back to the house and Laura sequestered them to their kennels. "This is not going to work. I'll have to call my friend and tell her to come pick them up. I can't handle their care." She sat in a dining room chair and covered her face with her hands. "I don't think I can take one more catastrophe." Dee Dee patted Laura on the back, but she looked at me like she needed me to throw her a life-line.

Laura removed her hands and looked at me with teary eyes. "Trixie, will you help me?"

I put myself in Laura's Dockers. "I'll do what I can. How about I talk with Edna and see what she can tell us?"

"If she worked for Grace all these years, she should be able to enlighten us if there are others who've had run-ins with her," Dee Dee said.

Mama walked up and placed her hand on Laura's shoulder. "Laura, what can I do for you?"

The waterworks started again. "Oh, Betty Jo. I don't know what to do." She sniffed and wiped her nose with a clean napkin. "Trixie and Dee Dee took pity on me and offered to interview Grace's housekeeper. If anyone knows Grace's secrets, Edna should."

"I'm so glad they've agreed to help. Trixie and Dee Dee have a knack for sniffing out the bad guys." She looked at me with a mother's love written all over her face. *Geeze, talk about a guilt trip.* I smiled back sweetly.

Father, you are going to have to help me on this one. It's way too big for me and Dee Dee.

"Dee Dee, let's take a walk and see if Edna can answer some questions."

"Okie dokie." Dee Dee grabbed a danish from the table before we left. "What? I'm still hungry."

"The least you can do is share." She tore off a small corner and handed it to me. I popped it in my mouth happy to get a morsel.

"Mmm." I licked the sugar off my fingers and wiped them on my pants. I know – not very dainty.

Ellie walked out the door behind us. "Hi. It's a beautiful day for a walk on the beach. I thought I'd get some exercise before lunch, then go site-seeing after we eat." We walked through the garden featuring a kaleidoscope of roses. Pink, red, yellow, and coral roses painted a colorful landscape. Rock walkways wound through the little bit of heaven on earth.

Ellie asked her own question. "What are you two ladies up to?"

Dee Dee piped up. "Oh, we're going over to ask Edna..." I grabbed Dee Dee's arm and gave it a hefty squeeze. She looked at me with raised eyebrows. I didn't want her to divulge our plans. The less people knew about our involvement the better.

"Yeah, we're going over to the Inn to see if Edna needs any help during this difficult time."

"What a wonderful idea. How about I go with you?"

I couldn't help but wonder if she was sincere about helping, or if she was just curious. "Thank you, Ellie, but you go ahead and take your walk. We don't want to overwhelm her." I crossed my fingers and hoped she'd decide to follow her original plans. We didn't need an extra set of ears around when we questioned Edna.

"Well, if you don't think you'll need me." I shook my head and watched her stroll toward the beach.

Dee Dee and I walked to the front of the bed and breakfast. I had to admit it was a cute cottage. The two story wood structure was painted coral with white trim, surrounded by a porch scattered with rockers. Swings hung at each end offering the weary traveler an invitation to rest.

Before we knocked, the door swung open. We jumped simultaneously. Bubba stood there, dressed in shorts and a tropical shirt dotted with colorful toucans. "Hi there, y'all. Come on in." *Had he been watching us?* He opened the screen door and motioned for us to enter. "Hasn't this been a terrible thing about Grace bein' murdered and all? Who would've thought winnin' the lottery would lead to bein' involved in a murder?" He shook his head like a wet dog. "No siree. I didn't know what I was gettin' into. I sure didn't sign up for this."

"Uh, Mr. Maxwell," Dee Dee said.

"Just call me Bubba. I don't stand on ceremony. Just because I'm a millionaire now I'm still country folk at heart. Money won't change that."

"Okay, Bubba. Is Edna here?"

"She sure is. I'll go get her for ya." He headed toward the back.

I took the breather to look around the room. It was absolutely beautiful. A huge rock fireplace covered one of the walls. Wicker furniture filled the room. The accent color was the same coral color painted on the outside. It shouted, "Welcome!" It was easy to see that Seaside Cottage and Ocean View Inn were both comfortable and welcoming places to stay. I could see where the defining factor could be the kindness and personality of the hostess. It could tip the scales one way or the other. If Grace had been as grouchy as Laura claimed, there was a good probability she ran off quite a few guests.

"Country boy's taking his time," Dee Dee said.

"Shhh, here they come."

"Here she is, ladies." Bubba's rotund frame hid Edna from view. "Well, I'm off to see the sights. Hope y'all have a good day." He bowed as far as his pouch allowed and went on his way to reveal the petite lady behind him.

"Hi, Edna." Dee Dee extended her hand. "I'm Dee Dee Lamont and this is Trixie Montgomery. We're staying at Seaside Cottage." Edna looked a little bewildered, but offered her hand to Dee Dee.

"What can I do for you? I'm sure you've heard the owner of Ocean View has passed away."

"Yes, and we're sorry for your loss." I didn't know how to approach this delicately so I charged ahead. "Look Edna, we're friends of Laura's and we'd like to ask you a few questions about Grace."

"I don't understand. Why do you want to know about Grace? That Detective Baker has already talked to me." She took a cloth tucked in her pocket and wiped off a glass tabletop.

"The truth is, Laura's been questioned and named a person of interest in Grace's murder. She's a long-time friend of my mother. Laura's devastated and my mother's asked us to see what we can find out. We thought since you knew her so well you'd be a good place to start."

She hesitated, weighing her words. "I know one thing for sure. That's one lady I ain't gonna miss."

CHAPTER TEN

Is there somewhere private we can talk?" I searched the room to see if any of the other guests lingered. I didn't see anyone, but didn't want to take a chance they were in listening distance.

"I have a small apartment off the kitchen. We can talk in there." Edna had taken a small area and made it into a comfortable living space, and small described the living area right enough. It consisted of one large open room with a double bed on one side of the room and a couch, small dinette table, and television on the other side. A tiny bathroom was located off to the side.

"How cute, Edna," Dee Dee said.

"Thank you. I've lived here for fifteen years. It's the only home I have." Edna plopped on the couch as if her legs wouldn't hold her up another minute. Tears glistened on her cheeks. "I'm sorry. I didn't mean to cry." She pulled a wadded up handkerchief from her pocket and wiped her eyes.

"Oh, don't worry. We all need a good cry every now and then." Dee Dee sat down beside her. "And under the circumstances, you have every reason."

I thought of all the times I'd boohooed on Dee Dee's shoulder. Even though she'd been through her own trials when her husband Gary died suddenly almost three years ago. I strived to follow her strength and faith.

Edna sniffed. "I'm not crying over her murder. That woman never caused anything but grief and sorrow to those who crossed her path." She blew her nose and emitted a sound akin to a pig snort.

"Did she make your life hard?"

Edna shot Dee Dee a look like she was plum crazy. "Hard? She made my life miserable. If I ever threatened to quit, which I did quite often, she said she would tell everyone I stole from her. She'd make sure I'd never work on the island again. Can you imagine what it was like to live under those circumstances?" We shook our heads in unison. She continued.

"I'm sorry about Ms. Laura being fingered for killing the old bat. I can't imagine her killing a fly. I'll help you in any way I can. As a matter of fact, if you do find out who did it I sure would like to shake their hand." She released a maniacal laugh. I wondered if the stress had made her a little uneven. Considering her giddy behavior, I easily pictured her knocking off Grace.

"Trixie? Edna asked you a question."

"Uh, sorry. What did you ask?"

"She asked what she could do to help. You know, with the investigation." Dee Dee shot me a questioning look.

"Oh. Right." I scooted to the edge of the chair. "Edna, could you give us a list of people who might have had a run-in with Grace in the past?"

Dee Dee rummaged around her gigantic purse and popped out a notepad and pen. I've never been with Dee Dee when she wasn't carrying a larger than life pocketbook, usually color coordinated with her outfit.

"Well, shoot. I expect you don't have enough paper in that little notebook of yours to write down all the names." Dee Dee and I exchanged glances. This wasn't going to be an easy task. "Now let me see." She looked up as if the names were written on the ceiling.

"The first person that pops into my mind is Mary Sue. She was a cook at Flounders, a local seafood restaurant."

"Do you know Mary Sue's last name?" Dee Dee's pen was poised ready to write.

"Sure, it's Bartlett. Mary Sue Bartlett. Anyway, Grace had it in for poor ole Mary Sue." She shook her head at Mary Sue's plight. "She used to help out here and I treasured her help as much as her friendship. Everything was fine until she took the job at Flounders." She had a far-away look in her eyes.

"What did her job have to do with Grace?"

"Well, that's just it. She had all these wonderful recipes she introduced at the restaurant. The dishes became big hits with the customers, and the owners promoted her to head chef. Before long, a producer invited her to host a local cooking show. She was ecstatic, and all her friends were happy for her.

"Of course, she quit her job here. I missed her, but was glad she wasn't stuck here like me. It wasn't long until the feathers started to fly. Grace found out that the recipes she'd been using at the restaurant and on the cooking show were ones Mary Sue had developed when she worked here. Grace had all new hires who worked in the kitchen sign a contract, and the fine print stated her recipes couldn't be shared outside the Inn. She claimed they were original family secrets, and she didn't want anybody else discovering the ingredients."

Dee Dee shook her hand as if she had a cramp, and caught my eye, her brow raised.

"I imagine Grace didn't take too kindly to that. But I don't see how she could prove they were her recipes. A lot of dishes are made with similar ingredients." Didn't sound like much of a case at this point.

"Grace could've let it go, but it wasn't her way. She hounded poor Mary Sue to death. She threatened a lawsuit. She literally stalked the woman. Eventually, Mary Sue couldn't take it anymore. She finally quit her job at the restaurant and the cooking show. Poor thing, she became so depressed there were times I thought she'd trip over her lip."

Dee Dee shoved the pad toward me. "You write. My hand is cramped up." I grabbed the items. "What happened to Mary Sue?"

"She wound up working at a fast food joint. She barely makes enough to feed herself and her kid. She was furious with Grace. Said she'd get even with her."

CHAPTER ELEVEN

That sure doesn't bode well for Mary Sue." I settled the notepad on my knee. "Do you know any other people who might have a burr under their saddle concerning Grace?"

"You better believe it. She collected enemies like most people collect seashells. Grace couldn't even keep a husband without running him off." My head popped up. Dee Dee shot me a glance.

I knew enough about murders to know that the spouse or ex-spouse is often the first person to be suspected. "Does he live around here?"

"I think it's somewhere in Savannah, but I'm not sure. They used to have the most awful knock-down, drag-out fights. They didn't seem to care who knew. They would argue right in front of the guests and God himself. I often wondered who would kill the other one first. Finally, he just up and left."

"Hmm, doesn't sound like they separated too amicably," Dee Dee said.

"That's the truth," Edna said.

"Edna, could you tell us what his name is?"

"Bert. Bert Watkins."

"Yoo hoo. Anybody home?" I knew that voice anywhere. Nana.

Edna jumped up. "Oh, my. I've neglected the guests too long. I need to go see about them. Please excuse me. I hope I've been some help to ya."

Dee Dee and I stood up and followed Edna to the kitchen.

There Nana stood, making herself at home. "Hi, Trixie. Betty Jo said

I could probably find you here." She twirled around in a circle. "Would you take a look at this kitchen? Every kind of cooking tool you could dream of."

An island with a marble countertop stood in the middle of the large kitchen. Copper pots and pans hung around the top of the island. An industrial-sized refrigerator and stove stood against the walls. A kitchen any woman would love to find in her home.

"Nana. Why were you looking for us?"

George came in and stood beside her. "I have the most wonderful news." She shot him a hundred watt smile. "George wants to take us to the Crab Shack tonight. It's supposed to have the best seafood on the island. All kinds of celebrities have eaten there."

George placed his arm around Nana's shoulder. "That's right, ladies. I've been told this establishment meets the highest of standards. I would love to be accompanied by a group of lovely ladies, if you will do me the honor."

"That sounds great. Don't you think so, Trixie?"

"Yes, I do. You won't see me turning down a good seafood meal. I've heard of the Crab Shack. They keep live alligators the customers can feed."

While we talked about the Crab Shack's fare, Edna returned to the kitchen. She walked over and addressed George. "Mr. Knight, I noticed you came out of Mr. Porter's room this morning. Were you lookin' for him?" For a fleeting second I thought I saw a look of anxiety cross George's face, but then it was gone just as quick.

"Yes, I was looking for John. Do you know where he might have gone? Or when he might get back? I have a matter I wish to discuss with him."

I wondered if he really wanted to talk with John Porter or if he had another motive. I liked George, but there was something about him that prompted me to keep an eye on him. I didn't want Nana hurt by the English Romeo.

"He returned from Seaside Cottage after breakfast, and then went out again. I haven't seen him since."

"No matter. I shall talk with him later." He turned from Edna and addressed us. "Ladies, I must take my leave for now and take care of some business. I look forward to seeing you tonight." He looked at Nana and smiled. "Belle, may I have the privilege of driving you to the restaurant this evening?"

I swanny, Nana turned crimson. "I'd be honored."

"Then I shall see you ladies around seven." He bowed at the waist. I had to admit, George was the consummate gentleman. Why did I keep getting prickly vibes about him? I wondered if I could solicit Beau to run a background check. Thinking of Beau sent a wave of sadness through me. I missed him. He'd promised me space to think about his proposal while I was gone, but it didn't keep me from missing him.

The shock of finding Grace's body and now trying to help Laura was more than I could handle. How could I contemplate my future? I knew I couldn't do this alone. *"Lord, please help me help Laura. And give me the wisdom to make the right decision about me and Beau."*

An overwhelming desire to talk to Beau struck me. I'd call him as soon as I had some alone time. I promised I'd have an answer for him when I returned. I loved Beau, but I couldn't let go of the seeds of fear my failed marriage had planted in me.

"Trixie?" Dee Dee shook me arm. "What were you thinking about, girl? You looked so serious."

I looked at Nana. How much should I divulge in front of her? I shouldn't have worried; she was far wiser than I gave her credit for. I thought of all the times she acted like she didn't know what was going on. I felt more than ever it was just a ruse for her to get away with her antics.

"Sugah, are you thinking about Beau?" Nana's eyes were filled with concern. I nodded. "I know you have a lot on you, but please don't forget how much he loves you. Anyway, if you don't marry Beau then that leaves him wide open for me." Nana and Dee Dee chuckled. Even though they laughed at my expense, Nana had lightened the mood. I gave her a big hug. Dee Dee joined in the fun as we enveloped each other in a group hug. Edna looked on as if we'd lost our ever lovin' minds.

When we were finished with our collective moment of encouragement, we turned to thank Edna for her help. "Oh goodness. I don't know how much I helped, but please let me know if you need me. I'll be glad to help Ms. Laura any way I can." She walked us to the door.

"Come on girls. Let's go tell Betty Jo we're going to the Crab Shack tonight. I've got a hot-looking outfit in mind that's sure to turn George's head."

"Nana!" *Oh, Lord, please deliver me.* Anyway, all she ever wore were jogging outfits.

"What? You don't think an old woman can look sexy?" Nana turned and strutted out the door.

Nana was going to be the death of me yet.

CHAPTER TWELVE

O h, Nana. I love you."

"I love you, too, Nana."

I knew Dee Dee meant it.

We found Mama resting in her room. That was, until Nana blew in like the north wind. "Oh, Betty Jo, we have the best news. George is going to take us to the Crab Shack tonight. Isn't that exciting?" Mama sat up. Nana walked over and plopped on the end of her bed.

"It sounds good." Mama shot a glance at me with a lifted eyebrow. "Trixie, what do you think? Should we go?"

I didn't see a need to tell her of my hunch about George. What could he do with four women in tow? "Sure. I think it'll be fun." Now seemed the perfect time to call Beau. "If y'all don't mind, I'd like to go find a quiet place and make a call."

Nana and Dee Dee exchanged a knowing gaze. "Sweetheart, you go on and call that hunk of gorgeous. It'll make you feel better."

I hoped she was right.

He answered on the second ring. "Hey, Babe."

"Hi. Is this a good time to talk?" Beau was a deputy sheriff in our small hometown of Vans Valley. I'm not sure why I felt like a kid calling her high school crush all of a sudden. I swallowed against a tiny giggle.

"Yeah, it's fine. I'm not busy right now. It's good to hear your voice." I could picture him leaned back in his office chair. "How are things going?"

I was torn. Should I tell him all I'd been through? With only a slight hesitation I spilled my guts. "Oh, Beau. It's been terrible. Monday night I went for a walk on the beach and found a dead body." The tears rolled down my cheeks. I took my sleeve and swiped at them.

"What?" I held the phone away from my ear, but it was too late. "Trixie, what have you been up to? I'm scared to let you out of my sight."

He had reason to be upset. After all, this was the third time I'd been involved in a murder investigation. But it wasn't my fault. And right now I needed him to empathize with me, not yell at me.

"I didn't know an innocent walk on the beach would lead me to a dead body," I said.

"I'm sorry. I shouldn't have yelled, but it caught me by surprise. You're there and I'm here, and I can't do anything to help. Did they interrogate you?"

"Yes. But Laura, Mama's friend, is the focus of the investigation. Grace Watkins, the victim, owned the bed and breakfast right next door to where we're staying. They had an ongoing argument and the murder weapon's a garden gnome Laura owns. She's asked me and Dee Dee to help her."

"Trixie." I could imagine Beau shaking his head.

"Beau, I have to help her. She's Mama's friend, and I'd want someone to do the same for me."

"I know, I know. That's who you are. But I'm worried about you. The last time you were involved in a murder investigation you barely made it out alive."

"Never fear. Nana's here and she's determined to help. Again."

"Is there anything I can do?"

I knew Beau would come at the drop of a hat if I wanted him to, but for now I needed information.

"Could you run a background check for me? Nana's got the hots for a gentleman named George Knight."

Beau's laughter rang through the phone. "I can't check on someone just because they want to date your grandma, hon."

"It's not just that." Although now that you mention it. "I've got this sense he's hiding something, but I can't put my finger on it."

He adopted his deputy sheriff voice. "Do you know his address? I could run his license plate number if you can get it."

"No, but we're going out tonight and I'll figure out a way to get it." My journalism skills came in handy for more than just scoops. "I'd feel better if I knew he was harmless." A knock on the door startled me. The door squeaked open and Dee Dee poked her head in.

"Is it all clear for me to come in?" she stage whispered. I nodded.

"Beau, Dee Dee just came in. I'm gonna let you go, but I'll call you back as soon as I get George's address." Dee Dee raised an eyebrow.

"Okay." His voice took on a husky tone. "It's so good to hear from you and I look forward to your next call. Trixie?"

"Yes."

"I love you."

"I love you, too, Beau." I knew he wanted me to say more, but I couldn't. I still had a lot to think over.

Dee Dee sat on my bed. "Wanna talk about it? I know you've got a lot on your mind." She looked me in the eye. "Trixie, follow your heart. Beau's a great guy. He loves you and he loves the Lord. That's a win-win combination."

"I know Dee. I'm scared." I couldn't help but think of the betrayal I'd lived through because of Wade's actions. I never wanted to experience that pain again.

"A little fear is healthy, Trix, but don't let the past prevent you from being happy. There are no guarantees in life, but remember, Beau is not Wade. Let's pray about it right now." Dee Dee clasped my hand and said the sweetest prayer. When we lifted our heads I felt a renewed peace.

"Thanks, Dee."

"You're welcome. Whose address were you talking about?"

"George's address. I can't put my finger on it, but there's something about him that bothers me. Did you hear Edna ask him about going in to John Porter's room this morning? I don't believe his explanation. We need to wheedle an address, at least get his license plate number. Beau said he could run a background check on him."

"That shouldn't be too hard. We'll work it into the conversation somehow." She patted my hand. "Hey, want to go downtown and check out the shops? We could stop by the fast food place where Mary Sue works and ask her some questions."

I sat up. "Let's check out the Seaside Sisters gift shop while we're out. Mary Kay Andrews leases a section in the store. She sells antiques and gifts."

"Oh, I just love Mary Kay's books. She's so funny."

"Did you notice the glass painting in the bathroom? Nancy Smith, one of the shop's founders, painted it. They're her specialty. I'd love to purchase one for my apartment."

Dee Dee nodded and shot me a grin. "Or maybe for your new house?"

I returned her smile and grabbed her arm. "Come on. Let's go participate in some retail therapy."

While I tied the laces on my Keds, my mind worked overtime coming up with a way to find out more about the mysterious George. And what exactly were his intentions toward Nana?

CHAPTER THIRTEEN

Tybee Island was a grand total of two and a half square miles of land. Located on Highway 80, the drive to Seaside Sisters didn't take long. The gift shop, housed in a small, older home, sat close to the road. Hand-made mobiles, flower pots, lawn ornaments, and even garden gnomes, decorated the outside. Dee Dee parked in the sandy yard of the little white and blue shop. We hopped out of the car and followed excited shoppers into the boutique.

"Oh, look, Trixie. Aren't these cute?" Dee Dee picked up a pint-sized canning jar, attached to a glass stem, and held up the drinking apparatus. "This is called Hillbilly Stemware." Other shoppers within earshot of Dee Dee's announcement smiled at the unique object.

I told Dee Dee she could find me in Mary Kay Andrew's corner, and headed straight for her space. Blindsided by some colorful jewelry, I stopped to sift through the fascinating trinkets, and picked out one for Mama and one for Nana. I wasn't disappointed when I finally found Mary Kay's area. I'd read about her love of antiquing and I knew she wove her adventures into her books.

The instant I spotted the cute little section filled with books, candles, and of course, antique furniture, I knew Dee Dee would adore it. She could choose from plenty of goodies to take back for her own emporium, Antiques Galore.

A middle-aged lady dressed in Dee Dee-like clothes struck up a conversation. "Are you from around here or just visiting?" She picked up a beautiful hand-made quilt and passed her hand back and forth over the lovely material.

"I'm from Vans Valley, a small town in north Georgia. My name's Trixie Montgomery." I picked up an outdoor mobile crafted from discarded kitchen utensils. Mama's yard would make a great home for the decoration. *Or maybe my yard?*

"Hi, I'm Ruth. Are you staying in one of the hotels on the beach or in Savannah?" She studied the price tag on the throw and quickly replaced it. She bestowed a couple of pats on the beautiful covering as if to say good-bye.

"Neither one. We're staying at Seaside Cottage."

Her eyes grew large and her jaw dropped. "Oh. I heard about Grace Watkins' death. Isn't it a shame they've arrested poor Laura for the murder?" I started to correct her, but she chattered without taking a breath. "I'm not surprised something like that happened to Grace. I'm a member of the Save the Turtles Association and she consistently rubbed someone the wrong way. Now that she's gone, I wonder if Jasmine will come back to the meetings. She'd never attend while Grace was alive."

My investigative antennas shot straight up. I wanted to ask more questions, but this wasn't the place. Too many people milled around.

Dee Dee walked up and eyed the mobile I held, tinkling above my head. "Hey, Trix. Did you find something to buy?"

"Yeah. Don't you think this is interesting?" She nodded. I turned toward my new acquaintance. "This is Ruth and we were discussing Grace Watkins."

Dee Dee's eyebrows lifted. "Oh?"

"Ruth, I'd love to hear more about the Grace and Jasmine situation. Could we meet later and talk?" I grabbed Dee Dee's arm and pulled her beside me. "We're trying to help Laura."

"Sure. I haven't eaten yet. Would you like to meet for lunch? There's a great little place right down the road. The Tybee Sandwich and Ice Cream Shop."

"Okay, as soon as we finish here we'll meet you. How about forty-five minutes?" We said our good-byes and I made it my mission to find the painted glass. I discovered several delightfully framed stained glass windows covered with brightly colored fish. I easily pictured one of these in my apartment.

"Look, Dee. Wouldn't this be great in my bathroom?" I held it up so Dee Dee could see the sun shining through the brightly painted windowpanes.

"Your apartment, or your new home with Beau?" Dee Dee stepped back a little like I might hit her. "Never mind. It'll look great in either one." Her beautiful smile was infectious. I smiled back.

We browsed the treasure trove a few more minutes and then paid for our purchases. My mind wandered while Dee Dee stored her packages in the back. I imagined being Beau's wife. He'd been nothing but good to me and I knew he loved the Lord. He'd endured similar circumstances in his first marriage as I had in mine. We'd both felt the brain-numbing effects of betrayal. Could we get past those feelings and build a trusting and loving marriage? *God, please help me make the right decision.*

"Hey, Trixie! Are you going to start the car?" She twisted around to straighten the items we'd bought.

Dee Dee's inquiry and her body leaning on my shoulder brought me back to earth. "Hold on to your pantaloons, girl." I said a silent prayer of thanks when my new car started on the first try.

As I drove through town, I noticed the shops on each side of the street. It was tourist heaven. Antique shops, gift shops, bakeries, and enough restaurants to please any palate lined both sides. And if you decided on a tattoo to commemorate your visit, The Pirate's Cove Tattoo Parlor would be glad to ink you up. I tried to imagine a pirate's skull or perhaps a turtle drawn on my old-lady ankle, but giggled to myself. What would Beau think?

"Stop!" Dee Dee yelled at the top of her lungs.

I slammed on the brakes and shot a glance in the rear view to see if the car behind us stopped. I stuck my finger in my ear, sure I'd be deaf the rest of my life.

"What? Are you trying to get us killed?" Another look in my review mirror alerted me a long line of cars followed us. Thank God the person behind us had quick reflexes.

"Over there. See it? A pirate." Dee Dee pointed out her side window.

Sure enough, a buccaneer stood on the sidewalk. Or rather, someone dressed like a water bandit. He wore an eye patch and a live parrot sat on his shoulder. I must admit he made a striking figure. A car horn blared a warning.

"Oh, good grief." Dee Dee turned around. I assumed she made a face at the offending culprit. "We're moving already."

"Well, are you happy now? You just about got us killed." I drove on down the street looking for the road Ruth told us to turn on.

"Pooh. We weren't in danger. You just over-reacted. Hey, do you think the peg leg was real?"

I gave Dee Dee a quick look. "You're kidding, right?" I worried about that girl sometimes. "I have to admit though, I was impressed. For a fake pirate, he looked authentic." I was wondering why he was dressed like a run-a-way from Treasure Island when Dee Dee supplied me with the answer.

"He was standing by a sign advertising a Pirate Festival. That sounds like fun."

"It does. Let's find out more about the festival. Keep a look out for Ocean View. Ruth said the restaurant is on the left."

While we looked for the turn, I speculated whether Ruth would feed us enough information about the mysterious Jasmine to add her to our growing list of suspects.

CHAPTER FOURTEEN

There's Ocean View!"

I swung a sharp right and spotted The Tybee Sandwich and Ice Cream Shop. "Where should I park?"

"There's a lot behind the building."

We parked, and walked around front. It was wonderful to walk without my cane and minimal pain. Now that I'd had my knee replacement I often wondered why I'd waited so long.

Like most establishments in Tybee, the sandwich shop boasted an ocean motif. Large fishing nets adorned the walls. A shelf covered in a variety of conch shells ran the perimeter of the room just below the ceiling. Numerous sea items decorated the walls: oars, antique ship wheels, compasses, and several mounted fish, including a huge blue and green sailfish. Some wise-guy had placed a fake bloody hand in the shark's mouth.

I spotted Ruth sitting in a corner booth. She waved us over and we scooted onto the bench opposite her.

"Hi. Did you have any trouble finding the restaurant?" She took our pocketbooks and placed them next to her giving us more room.

"Not at all. We did see a pirate, though." Dee Dee scanned a menu.

"The Pirate Festival is an annual event Tybee hosts to attract tourists during the off season. It's great fun. There's a parade where everyone dresses up in a pirate-themed costume and walks downtown. A king and queen are crowned. It's fun if you like that kind of arr-ful entertainment."

"Won't Nana like that?"

I gave Dee Dee a stern look. "Don't even think about getting her involved in a pirate festival."

"Ha! You know she'll find out one way or the other. She might as well join in the fun." Dee Dee could afford to laugh. Nana wasn't her responsibility. Last year in Marietta, we attended a Civil War Ball and Nana dressed like Scarlett. She got into the character so much she insisted she was really Scarlett. Just about drove me crazy.

"You're right, but don't encourage her."

A waitress, outfitted in a pirate themed white dress and black apron, approached our table. "Hi. May I take your order?" I hadn't even looked at the menu.

"Ruth, do you have any suggestions?"

"Try the fish filet sandwich with fries and salad. I think you'll like it."

I handed the waitress my menu. "I'll take that, please."

"I'll have the same thing," Dee Dee said. The cute waitress wrote down our order and sashayed toward the kitchen.

Ruth looked around, placed her elbows on the table, and leaned in toward us. "Can you tell me what you had in mind when you suggested we meet?"

"Could you tell us about Jasmine? What happened to cause so much dissension between Grace and Jasmine?"

Dee Dee elbowed a warning. After the waitress set down our drinks and left, Ruth continued.

"It's a long story, but I'll try to give the short version. As you know, Grace is an icon in the community. I mean was, bless her heart. I think she must have been one of the founding fathers." Ruth gave a nervous little laugh at her own joke. "Anyway, Jasmine was a newcomer to Tybee and a pretty young thing at that.

"Grace had been the president of Save the Sea Turtles for as long as I can remember. When it came time to vote for new officers, Jasmine had the audacity to run against her. Nobody, and I mean nobody, dared to run against Grace. She's been unopposed for years." She stopped to take a breath and glanced around again, as if she thought Grace might walk through the door any minute.

"I guess Grace didn't take too kindly to Jasmine?" Dee Dee took a long sip from her sweet tea, let out a big "ahhh," and set her glass back down.

"Ha! That's an understatement. Grace was out for blood. I don't know how she did it, but she dug up all the dirt she could on Jasmine, and then made sure everyone in the club knew about it."

"What did she discover that was so awful?" I was beginning to get a feel of just how mean and spiteful Grace had been.

"She'd made some bad decisions when she was young. We've all done things in our youth we wish we could go back and change. Grace found out Jasmine served time in jail for possession of marijuana. Even though it had been over fifteen years, members didn't want someone with a record for their president."

Another waitress returned with our orders. The food looked and smelled delicious.

"Wow, get a gander at these sandwiches. They're Papa Bear size." Dee Dee was right. The portions were the largest I'd seen. Steak fries covered three-fourths of the plate. We took a few minutes to doctor with condiments waiting on the table.

"Mmm, this is good." A glob of tartar sauce oozed out on the corner of Dee Dee's mouth. I pointed to my mouth to clue her in. She shot us an embarrassed look and wiped off the offending sauce. Quiet enveloped our table while we tamed our hunger. Once sated, we talked between bites.

"Ruth, what did Jasmine do when she wasn't allowed to run?" I dipped a crispy fry in a lake of ketchup and popped it in my mouth.

"She was madder than a pirate who'd lost his booty. Jasmine stood up at the meeting and told Grace she was going to put a stop to her antics. Then she just walked out. I haven't seen her at another meeting." Ruth pushed her empty plate away.

"Ladies, would you like dessert?" Our lady pirate offered dessert menus.

"I don't know. I'm full as a tick." I patted my belly to prove it.

Dee Dee elbowed me. "Hey, speak for yourself." She pointed to a picture on the menu. "Look at this." She jabbed her finger at a chocolate dessert. "Pirate's Booty. I'll have this please."

My mouth watered. "Wanna share?"

"I don't think so." Dee Dee looked at me like I'd lost my mind. Ruth said she'd share with me so we ordered two Pirate's Booty double chocolate desserts. Oh well, what's a girl to do? After all, we were on vacation.

We sat back to wait. "Ruth, can you tell us how we could get in touch with Jasmine?"

CHAPTER FIFTEEN

She works at one of the local tourist shops, Pirate's Treasure. She's listed in the phone book as Jasmine Watters."

"Dee Dee, are you getting this down?" She nodded as she wrote in her notebook.

The waitress returned with our desserts. I cut mine in half and handed Ruth a portion. Dee Dee stuck her finger in the icing and plopped the gooey sweetness into her mouth. "Mmm. Aren't you glad you ordered your own?"

The next few minutes were quiet except for a few mmms and aahs as we devoured the scrumptious treat. We thanked Ruth for her help and said our good-byes.

"The list grows longer," Dee Dee noted.

"Who's on the roll so far?"

Dee Dee retrieved her notebook and shoved it toward me. "Take a gander."

1. Mary Sue Bartlett – Grace's former cook.
2. Bert Watkins – Grace's ex-husband.
3. Jasmine Watters – wanted to run for president of Save the Turtles.

"Dee I know we don't have George written down. I mean there's no need for him to be on the list, but I still have qualms about him."

I drove back toward the Inn.

Dee surveyed our list of suspects. "We can't forget to find out his address and tag number tonight so Beau can run a background check on him."

I had an idea and slowed to make a turn. "Let's take a detour and check out the lighthouse."

"Sounds good to me. Your camera's in the backseat if you want pictures."

She reached back and grabbed it for me.

"Savannah and Tybee Island are steeped in history and I'm excited about the chance to write about some of the sights." I'd almost forgotten my writing assignment with the murder investigation.

I parked in the sandy lot and we walked across the road to join the other curious tourists. A family with three children in tow walked around the lighthouse. The man took pictures as they posed by the giant structure. I ran my hand over the historic plaque and read it out loud.

"A lighthouse on Tybee was one of the first public structures in Georgia. It was completed in 1736 by William Bilthman, built of cedar piles and brickwork." I continued to read aloud. My heart skipped a beat when I read Union soldiers burned it down. Years later, renovation would restore it to its original grandeur. I snapped picture after picture.

"We need to bring Nana and Mama to see this."

"That's a great idea." I clicked a few more pictures before we left.

We drove back to Seaside Cottage without incident, but if I'd known what awaited us I'd have driven the other way. I swanny, Nana was going to turn my locks gray one hair at a time.

She met us at the door. "Hi, girls. What 'cha been up to? Betty Jo and I have been on our own adventure."

I expected her to say na-na-na boo-boo any minute.

"You should see what I bought to wear tonight. George is going to be in for a treat."

Mama walked into the room. Her hair was uncombed and her clothes askew. She looked like she'd been through the wringer. "I'm so glad you're back. I need to rest for a while. Could you can keep Nana company?"

I gave Mama a questioning look. It all became crystal clear when Nana dropped her surprise on us.

"Look what I got." She lifted the pant leg of her jogging outfit, flooring me.

"Nana! A tattoo! Why in the world would you want to get a mermaid tattooed on your ankle?" I glanced over at Mama. I couldn't believe she agreed to Nana's indulgence.

Mama held out her hands, palms up. "We were shopping for something new to wear when she slipped away from me."

"Now, Betty Jo, don't you worry about this. I'm plenty old enough to make decisions for myself. I've always wanted a tattoo, and when I saw the Inked Tattoo Parlor, I thought *why not*? A mermaid is perfect to remember our trip by."

I loved Nana, but I knew her antics took a heavy toll on Mama. When Mama was a little girl she had lost both of her parents and Nana had stepped in to raise her. She loved her like a mother. Now the tables were turned, and Mama felt like she was the parent. I tried to imagine what it was like to be in Nana's shoes. She was plenty old enough to make her own decisions, but she didn't always make the best ones. I've tried to tell Mama, in Nana's case "you need to pick your battles." I guess Mama lost this one.

"I'm going upstairs to take a nap. Nana, why don't you come with me?" Mama looked like she would drop any minute.

"I'm not tired. Come on, Trixie. Let's go sightseeing."

"Nana, how about we all take a nap? You want to be fresh for George tonight, don't you?"

"Fresh? Of course I'll be fresh with George." Nana laughed at her own wit. I rolled my eyes.

"I saw that, Missy. Don't think you can sneak an eye roll by me." Nana has an uncanny sense of knowing when I do that, even if we're talking on the phone. "Okay, I'll retire for a nap if all of you are going to rest, too."

I no sooner put my head on the pillow when Dee Dee shook me. "Come on, Sleeping Beauty. It's time to get up. You don't want to be late for our big date tonight." I rolled over and pulled the covers over my head. Dee Dee promptly pulled them off. I slowly made my way from the bed to the bathroom. I returned to find Dee Dee ready to go.

I'd always heard if you have red hair there are certain colors you shouldn't wear. Dee Dee has never followed this rule. Today was no exception. She wore a bright orange jumper covered in yellow starfish. She'd complimented the outfit with a yellow short-sleeved shirt under the jumper. A yellow and orange necklace laced with seashells hung around her neck. She completed her outfit with a comfortable pair of Hush Puppies. She looked stylish and cute as she twirled around.

I settled on a pair of black slacks with a white button up blouse. I needed comfortable shoes for supporting my knee. I slipped on a pair of black Clarks. I stuck my left hand in front of me and peered at my empty ring finger. Would I have an engagement ring on the naked finger in a few days?

"Hey, what are you doing?" Dee Dee startled me.

"Uh, nothing." I changed the subject. "Wow. You look great. I need to add some color to my wardrobe."

"I've been telling you that for some time now."

I took one last glance in the mirror and recalled a necklace Beau had given me. I dug in my makeup bag and found it. A black butterfly hand-painted on the surface of a sand dollar was the perfect touch. *Not too bad.* I wished Beau could see me. I missed him and my heart ached. *God, please help me to make the right decision. Soon.*

I grabbed Dee Dee's arm and pulled her toward the door. "Come on, girlfriend. Let's go see what Nana's wearing."

CHAPTER SIXTEEN

This was the first time in several years I'd seen Nana decked out in a dress on a day other than Sunday. "Nana! You look gorgeous."

"Don't I though?" She twirled in her new outfit. "Do you think George will like it?"

"He'll love it." Dee Dee modeled for Nana. "What do you think of this?"

"Well, it won't be hard to find you when it's time for Cinderella to leave the ball." Dee Dee laughed and gave Nana a hug. It warmed my heart to see how patient Dee Dee was with Nana. I knew from experience that patience became a rare commodity after spending much time with her.

The front door opened and George stuck his head in. "Anybody home?"

Nana ran to the door and threw it open. George studied Nana and rewarded her with a whistle. She turned around for him and grinned ear to ear.

"You ladies ready?"

"Yes."

"Let's go."

"I'm ready."

A chorus of voices answered. We followed George to his car. Nana sat in front while the rest of us squeezed in the back. We had directions to the Crab Shack, but we made several wrong turns before we discovered the hidden restaurant. The parking lot was full; we hoped it was an indication of a good place to eat. I grabbed my camera and brought it along to snap pictures for the family album.

George put our name in for a table. We sat on comfortable seats, surrounded by other tourists, and waited. I looked around at the motif. Sea creatures covered the walls, along with anything connected to the ocean. I watched a family of four laughing and joking with each other. It appeared that every table accommodated people having a good time. I was glad George had invited us to tag along with him and Nana. Which reminded me, I needed to covertly get the information Beau needed.

In about fifteen minutes the waiter seated us and handed out menus. They were adorned with colorful sea critters drawn as cartoon-ish characters.

Nana commented. "Aren't these the cutest menus you've ever seen?" Then everyone started talking at the same time.

"Look at all the selections."

"I can't decide what I want."

"Look at this. They have Snow Crab, Alaskan King Crab, Blue Crabs, Dungeness Crabs, and Stone Crabs. A crab for every palate," Dee Dee said.

We talked back and forth several minutes before we decided on our fare. The waiter took our orders. We sat back, relaxed and ready for a good time. After orders were taken, I popped the question.

"George, where did you say you lived? I know Nana would love to exchange addresses so she could keep in touch with you."

"Oh, that's a great idea." Dee Dee threw in her two cents.

He took a long sip of his tea. Was he avoiding the question or weigh-ing what he wanted to say? "Uh, I travel a lot. My home is in Ohio, but I don't stay put much. How about I write down my post office box and give it to you later?" He revealed he worked in insurance, but when I tried to get detailed information he deftly changed the subject. Dee Dee wasn't any more successful.

Quicker than I expected, our waiter appeared with the food. He spread a feast before us: crab, shrimp, oysters, and mussels, with sides of smashed potatoes, corn, and slaw. Laughter and relaxed talk flowed easily around the table.

Nana's blue eyes widened. "I felt something on my foot!"

"Oh! I think I feel it!" Dee Dee reached under the table. Within the next minute pandemonium broke loose. Dee Dee emitted a blood-curdling scream. She lifted her hand up with a lobster attached.

"Help, help!" Her face turned bright red to match the color of the crustacean. She spun around in circles and slung her hand back and forth. Proving too much for the critter it turned loose and flew through the air.

What happened next will live in infamy. What are the odds out of all the people in the Crab Shack, a lady easily described as fluffy, decided to choose that moment to bend over to retrieve something from the floor. With her south side pointing north the lobster grabbed on to her plush derriere. A scream to rival Dee Dee's filled the room.

A man, dressed in chef's attire, ran into the room. "Oh, I'm so sorry. Please forgive me. A giant lobster escaped the kitchen and we couldn't find it." He ran over to the lady with the lobster hanging from her backside. He reached out to grab the lobster when the lady turned around and hit him with her pocketbook.

"Don't you dare touch me."

Wide-eyed he looked around for anyone to help him. Someone, I assume from her party, grabbed the lobster and pulled as hard as he could. Finally the lobster let go and the man went flying to the floor holding the prized lobster in his hand. The chef retrieved the delinquent lobster and hurriedly retreated to the kitchen.

The customers' first reaction was shock, but shortly everyone doubled over in laughter. Dee Dee didn't laugh. "Hey, that hurt. I'll never look at lobster the same."

"Better you than me," Nana said.

Everyone was too full for dessert, so we went outside and walked around. I clicked picture after picture of Nana feeding the 'gators. By the time we arrived back at Seaside Cottage we were exhausted. George bade us good-night and left.

"Girls, I'm ready to hit the hay. This has been too much excitement for me in one day. Let's hope tomorrow is more peaceful." Mama had no idea what was in store for us over the coming days.

Laura walked into the room. "How was your evening out?"

Mama gave her the short version and promised to fill her in tomorrow as we climbed the stairs, exhausted and ready for sleep.

Dee Dee exited the bathroom dressed in orange pajamas covered with black cats. She reminded me of a pumpkin. I couldn't help but laugh.

"And what's so funny?" She pulled on the sides of her pajama top. "Surely you're not laughing at my kitties?"

"No, no." I crossed my fingers and silently asked for forgiveness. "Do you think George avoided my question about his address?"

"Yeah. He hesitated too long. You seem to have struck a nerve." We talked for a while about the names on our suspect list and the best way to interview them. It was around midnight when we finally went to sleep. Way too early the next morning, Mama burst into our room and shook me awake.

CHAPTER SEVENTEEN

T rixie. Wake up." I rolled over and wiped the sleep from my eyes. Dee Dee rose up and propped herself up on her elbow.

"What is it, Mama? Is Nana alright?"

"Nana's fine, but Detective Baker took Laura down to the police department again. I'm worried sick about her." Mama's hair stuck out in all directions and her housecoat was turned inside out. "What are we going to do?"

I yawned. "Don't worry, Mama. He's probably just asking her some questions and then he'll bring her back home. I don't think they'll keep her."

"I feel terrible sitting here not able to do a thing to help her." She pulled at some loose strings on her robe. "I know she'd do what she could to support me."

Dee Dee spoke through the haze of sleep. "Trixie, tell her about the names we've come up with so far." Mama offered me a quizzical look.

"We've questioned some of the locals and came up with a list of people who might have it in for Grace. It seems she didn't mind meddling in other's lives when it was to her advantage. According to those who knew her well, she didn't give a hoot about hurting others." I shuddered thinking someone cared so little for the feelings of another human being.

"Can I see the list?" Mama smoothed her hair. Color returned to her cheeks. If it gave her hope to look over the names I didn't see any reason why she shouldn't.

Dee Dee threw back the covers, pushed her feet into her kitty slippers and padded over to her pocketbook. "I'll get it. I think I stashed it in here." She dug in her bag and came up with the notebook. She raised it in the air. "Ta-da." Dee Dee handed me the tablet and then settled on her bed, cross-legged.

I glanced at the names when the door flew open and Nana burst in. "What are you girls up to? How could y'all leave me out of the party?" If her lip drooped any lower she'd have to carry it in a wheelbarrow.

"Good morning to you too, Nana."

She gazed downward under hooded eyes. "Oh, good morning."

"We're not having a party. Detective Baker took Laura downtown again. Trixie was fixin' to go over the names of some suspects she and Dee Dee have compiled," Mama said.

"Well, what are you waiting on? I'm here now, so you can start." I started to roll my eyes but thank goodness I caught myself just in time. I didn't feel like an early morning lecture from Nana.

Nana looked me directly in the eyes. "Don't even think about it, Missy." *Good grief! How does she do that?*

Mama scooted close to me so she could see and Nana plopped down on my other side. "Let's see. There's Mary Sue Bartlett."

"She used to work for Grace as a cook and housekeeper." Dee Dee chimed in.

I continued. "She left Grace for a position at a downtown restaurant and before she knew it she had her own local cooking show. She thrived, until Grace accused her of stealing her recipes. Edna said Grace stalked Mary Sue and threatened to sic her lawyers on her. She freaked out and quit the restaurant. She waitresses in a fast food place now. She barely makes enough to support her daughter."

Dee Dee shook her head.

"Low-down, good for nothing…"

"Nana. Be careful."

"I was only going to say skunk. Actually that's too nice for her. I'll have to think of something else." I had no doubt she would.

"She certainly has reason to dislike Grace, but who else is on your list?" Mama leaned over and took a gander at the names.

"Edna's been Grace's head cook and house-keeper for the past fifteen years. Laura told us she knew Edna was unhappy. I don't think Laura had any idea how miserable Edna really is. When we mentioned her death she said, 'That's one lady I ain't gonna miss.'

"Why in the world would she stay?" Mama repositioned beside me.

"That's a good question. We wondered that, but she cleared it up when she said Grace threatened to blackball her. She told Edna if she left, she would never work on Tybee Island again. Since Edna makes her home with Grace, there wasn't much she could do about it. She felt stuck."

"Shoot, if Grace wasn't dead I think I could kill her myself." I knew Nana was kidding, but what a sad commentary for someone's life when no one would miss you.

"You can understand why we put Edna on the list. She had plenty of reasons to want Grace dead. When we talked with her she certainly didn't seem like a killer, but people have been known to kill for less," Dee Dee said.

Mama scrunched up her face. "Is that all the names you have?"

"No. It seems Grace made a lot of enemies, including her ex-husband, Bert. Edna shared how they used to have these awful fights in front of the guests. She was even afraid one of them would kill the other one. She said he just up and left one day - moved to Savannah.

"Grace got the better end of the deal, financially. If that's not a recipe for murder, I don't know what is."

Nana grabbed hold of the notebook and pulled it to herself. She pointed at a name scrawled near the bottom. "Who is this Jasmine?"

Dee Dee filled her in. "We met this really nice lady, Ruth, at Seaside Sisters. She invited us to eat lunch with her. She was full of gossip – I mean information."

"That's right. She couldn't wait to spill the beans. Jasmine, a young lady with the Save the Turtles Association, tried to run for president against Grace. It was a decision that turned out to be a big mistake in the end." I drew in a deep breath and continued.

"According to Ruth, Grace dug deep until she found dirt on Jasmine. Her contacts found out that Jasmine had been arrested for marijuana possession. Even though it was a misdemeanor and she never had to serve time, the rules of the association state you can't run if you have any kind of criminal record."

Nana shook her head.

Dee Dee scooted to the edge of her bed. "Yeah, and Jasmine was so mad she vowed to get even with Grace. She threatened her in front of the entire group of turtle savers. She definitely earned her place on the list of suspects."

CHAPTER EIGHTEEN

When are we going to talk to them, Trixie?" Watery blue eyes from behind thick lenses stared straight at me. I knew Nana was serious as a hound following a scent.

"Uh." I cleared my throat and looked at Dee Dee to throw me a lifeline. She shrugged her shoulders and raised her eyebrows. I was sinking fast. "Dee Dee and I have this covered, Nana. Maybe you can keep your ears open over at Ocean View Inn when you visit George."

"What can I do?" Mama tugged her housecoat a little tighter around her.

"Mama, you can keep your ears open, too. I think all the guests at Grace's could be considered suspects. We know they all had opportunity. What we need to find out is if they have a motive."

"Let's add them each to the list," Dee Dee suggested. She rummaged around in her pocketbook for a pen and handed it to me.

"Throw out names and I'll write them down." I poised my hand ready to write.

Everyone spoke at once. I threw up my hand, palm turned out. "Whoa. One at a time. Mama, who did you say?"

"What about Bubba Maxwell? He seems nice enough, but he kinda' gets on my nerves."

"Huh," Dee Dee said. "He gets on everybody's nerves. If he won the lottery like he says he did, then the motive wouldn't be money."

"There might be something in his past we don't know about. We have to find a way to uncover any motives." I wrote down his name.

"There's that sweet young couple KiKi and Nick Sanderson. You know, the cute kids that are tatted up." Great. All we needed was Nana spouting 'hood speak.' An image appeared in my mind of Nana covered in tattoos from head to toe. Believe me, it was not pretty.

"We need to write them on the list, too. At this point, no one is exempt. Even the guests here at Seaside."

Dee Dee returned from the bathroom and plopped down on her bed. "Where are we?"

"We were talking about that sweet couple, KiKi and Nick." Nana pushed her glasses up her nose.

"Oh, don't you just love their tattoos? What I'd give to be young again." Dee Dee had this faraway look in her eyes.

"Like you'd be covered in ink if you were?" *Please.* What was happening to everyone? Did the salt air addle their brains?

Dee Dee turned a little pink. "Well, no. But it never hurts to dream about 'what if.'"

Dee Dee thought a moment. "That leaves John Porter and George."

"George? Why in the world would you mention him?" Nana nearly choked on her indignation. "He's the nicest man you'd ever want to meet."

I shot Dee Dee a look that meant, 'way to go.' She just shrugged.

"Nana we need to consider everybody. I'm sure we'll find George is squeaky clean." I felt guilty for the doubts that clouded my mind concerning George.

"What about that man, John Porter?" Mama leaned over and tapped her finger on my notebook. "Write his name down."

"He seems like a decent enough guy, but he didn't have much to say when he came to the inn to eat." I pictured the fortyish, tall, dark and handsome man. I wondered what circumstances in his life landed him on Tybee Island at this particular time.

Dee Dee sported a starry-eyed glaze. "I wonder if he's married." Absentmindedly she fanned herself with the covers.

"Earth to Dee Dee!"

She snapped out of her daydream.

"Oh. Sorry. You have to admit he is one handsome hunk of humanity." She looked around the room for affirmation.

"You got that right," Nana heartily agreed.

"Okay, ladies." I brought the meeting back to order. "We need to get our focus off John Porter's hunky body and back on our suspects.

"Can you read the names again? Maybe we've forgotten someone crucial." Dee Dee stood up and stretched.

"Let's see.

1. Mary Sue Bartlett
2. Bert Watkins
3. Jasmine Watters
4. Edna Jackson
5. George Knight
6. Bubba Maxwell
7. Kiki and Nick Sanderson
8. John Porter

"Wow, what a list. How are you ever going to check out everyone?" Mama's face reminded me of a sunflower with no sun. "Trixie, I'm so afraid for Laura."

I gave Mama a big hug. "When Dee Dee and I released it to the One who does know all the answers before, He always came through, and I feel confident he'll see us through this, too."

Dee Dee and Nana offered a hearty, "Amen!"

"Don't forget the Daniels, Cassie and Harold. Then there's Ellie Sloan. Those are the only guests here besides us. Of course, there's Louise, but I can't see her harming a fly."

A knock on the door startled us, and we looked at each other like we'd done something illegal instead of collaborating on Laura's defense.

Dee Dee was closest so she grabbed the doorknob and eased the door open.

Laura stood on the other side. Dee Dee clutched her arm and pulled her in, guiding her inside to sit on the bed.

Mama sat beside Laura. When she gave her a hug tears began to pour from Laura's red-rimmed eyes. "Oh, Betty Jo. What am I going to do?" She sniffed and wiped her nose with her hand.

Nana pulled out a fairly fresh Kleenex from her bathrobe pocket. "Here dear."

We exchanged glances while she blew into the Kleenex sounding like a foghorn. A short time ago, Mama had been the one worried about Laura. It's amazing to see what one will do for a friend. She put on her big girl panties along with a forced smile and told Laura about the list of suspects we'd acquired. We took turns giving Laura a hug and words of encouragement. By the time we finished, she'd wiped her tears and girded a cloak of courage.

"Y'all come on down and have some breakfast." Laura had pulled herself together, and seemed encouraged that we had her back. "Louise said it'd be ready in a few minutes. I have another bit of good news to pass on. Grace's niece arrived last night, so I don't have to worry about her guest's care. As if I didn't have enough to worry about."

Laura went downstairs to check on Louise, and Mama and Nana went back to their room to change clothes.

"How are we going to interview all these people?" Dee Dee motioned at the list I still clutched. "You're not officially working, so you can't use that as an excuse."

"That's not exactly true. I'm not working on a particular article, but I am collecting research while I'm here to use later on. I don't see why I can't do the same with interviews."

"Trixie, we need to be careful. One murder's already been committed. I don't want one of us to be next."

CHAPTER NINETEEN

I wore my usual khakis paired with a teal short sleeve tee. Dee Dee dressed in jeans with a bright pink shirt and a cute matching scarf. A myriad of colorful bracelets jangled on her wrists. Her sneakers matched her top. Even though Dee Dee shopped in the Womens' section, she didn't let her size stop her from being stylish. I envied her confidence to wear fun colors and kicky new styles.

I raised the blinds and glanced toward the beach. A little ways beyond the fence a man and woman stood talking. I squinted to see if I could identify them. I thought I recognized Ellie, but wasn't sure about her companion.

"Dee, come here. See if you can figure out who's talking with Ellie."

She placed her face against the pane, her breath fogging up the window. "It looks like that man staying at Ocean View Inn."

"John Porter?" I hip bumped her aside so I could take another gander. "It does look like him. What in the world are they talking about? They look like a couple of seagulls trying to take flight."

"If I moved my arms that fast my skin would flap in the wind and I'd be in danger of knocking myself out. Let's corner her at breakfast and get some answers." Dee Dee grabbed her oversized tote and a sweater.

"Okay, let's go." I grabbed the suspect list, and shut the door.

"What's on our agenda besides interviews?" Dee Dee called over her shoulder as she descended the stairs.

"Why don't we drive to town? They're having an arts and crafts festival today, and then tomorrow night they host the Swashbuckler's Bash. Everyone dresses up and parties under a big tent. Think we should go?"

"Sure. Might as well have fun while we're investigating. Think we can escape without Nana finding out?"

I shook my head. "I doubt it. Nana never misses a beat."

Nana appeared from nowhere. "Were you talking about me?"

"Nana! You scared me to death. Took at least ten years off my life."

"Aw, don't exaggerate, Trixie." Nana hooked arms and walked with me to the dining room. "You're just feeling guilty because I caught you."

"We weren't exactly talking about you Nana. We were discussing the big pirate festival tomorrow night and your name came up," Dee Dee said.

I can't believe she told Nana about the festival. There go our plans. I reached over and pinched a healthy wad of flesh on Dee Dee's arm.

Her recently waxed eyebrows raised in an arch. "Ouch, what did you do that for?" She rubbed the offended area. Realization hit and her eyes opened wide. "Oh, I'm sorry. I guess it's too late to stuff the cat back in the bag?"

"Tell me more about this pirate festival. Sounds like something I'd love to attend." Nana shuddered with excitement. "Let's go tell Betty Jo."

I looked at Dee Dee. "Yep, too late."

Dee Dee shrugged. "Don't worry about Nana. I'll help you keep an eye on her. You'll see. It won't be so bad."

Yeah, famous last words.

We stepped into a dining room amid wonderful aromas. I grabbed a plate and filled it with bacon, eggs, hotcakes and various pastries. No such thing as calorie counting on vacation. Ellie was sitting alone and I made a beeline for her table. This would be the perfect time to question her. "Is this seat taken?"

"No. Please join me." She moved her utensils so I'd have room for my plate.

"Hey, Dee Dee! Over here." I motioned for her to join us.

Dee Dee's plate harbored a hearty breakfast, too. No skimping on our watch. She pulled out a chair and sat across from me.

"Hi." She eyed Ellie's plate of muffins, fruit and yogurt. "No wonder you stay so slim." Ellie's face turned a pretty shade of pink. She was a lovely girl. I wondered what if any role she played in Grace's murder.

"Ellie. Tell us about the Save the Turtles Convention. I know Grace was the president of the Tybee chapter. Are they still going to hold the meeting?" I shoveled a fork full of eggs in my mouth.

"That's a good question, Trixie. I've talked with some of the other attendees and the organizers are going ahead as scheduled. The local members planned a memorial for Grace on the last day. Even though she had the personality of a riled up porcupine, she contributed so much to saving the sea turtles. She's a legend in her own right." Ellie took a tiny bite of muffin – probably bran.

"Too bad she had to ruin her good works with her surly nature. Seems she cared more about turtles than she did humans." Dee Dee waggled her fork.

"Do y'all remember the argument Laura and Grace had the first day we arrived? Do you think that Laura really killed her?" Ellie appeared much too happy about Laura's troubles.

"No, we don't. That's why we're helping her." Dee Dee turned to me for assistance.

"That's right. Ellie could you tell us where you went the night I found Grace's body?"

Her green eyes opened wide and she stumbled over her next words. "Uh, I went into town. Don't you remember? I spent time at the Pirate's Pub with some of my friends attending the convention." Something about her answer seemed a little too contrived, but her response would be easy enough to check out. I decided to go for broke and charged ahead with the next question. "We saw you talking with John Porter this morning on the beach. Where do you know him from?"

She squinted at me, then turned to Dee Dee. "Ladies, I don't believe my personal life is any of your business." She scooted her chair back. "This conversation is over."

"Wow," Dee Dee exclaimed, watching her bolt out of the room. "If she doesn't have anything to hide she sure has a funny way of showing it."

"I agree. She might not be guilty of murder, but she's hiding something."

CHAPTER TWENTY

I stacked up our dirty dishes and scooted my chair back. Dee Dee grabbed a pile as well and we headed to the kitchen, still discussing Ellie's hasty departure.

Louise stood at the sink, up to her elbows in sudsy water. "Hey, ladies. Thanks for bringing the plates. Just set them on the drain board."

Checking to make sure we were alone, I thought this would be a great time to talk to her. "Louise, do you know Edna very well?"

"We've known each other over ten years. She's been working for Grace for fifteen and I've been with Laura for ten. We hit it off right away. I guess having so much in common made it easy to become friends."

Dee Dee pulled out a chair for me and picked up the line of questioning. "Did she ever talk about how Grace treated her?"

Louise rubbed her nose with her arm, leaving a wad of bubbles on the end of her snout. "She sure did. There wasn't any love lost between them two. Grace treated Edna like a mat to wipe her feet on. She cried on my shoulder more than once. But she was stuck. She doesn't have any family since she never married and her folks passed. At the time, it made sense to live with Grace. After a few years, things weren't so rosy anymore. Any time she talked about leaving, Grace threatened to blacklist her. Told her she'd never work on Tybee again. She had poor Edna scared half to death." Louise pointed to the dishes. "Could you hand me another stack, dear?"

Dee Dee gathered up a precariously high mound and carried them to the sink. The work keeping a bed and breakfast was never ending.

"We're doing everything we can to help Laura." Dee Dee assured Louise, and pulled the notebook from her pocket. "We have a list of people we want to question. Could you look it over and tell us where we might find some of them?"

"Honey, you're going to have to hold it way back if you expect me to read it." Dee Dee made the adjustment. "Whoa. That's a long list. You have Edna on the list? If I'd known that I wouldn't have told you all that stuff about her."

"No. No. Don't worry about Edna. We put everyone down that had recent contact with Grace. It doesn't mean we really suspect them of any wrong doing," Dee Dee said.

Louise was right, though. She had divulged a lot of information and it didn't bode well for Edna.

She placed her dripping hand under her chin, reminding me of The Thinker. "You can probably find Mary Sue at her job. She works at the local hamburger joint, Dairy Delite. The building's located on the main road right before you get into town. You can't miss it. Bert lives somewhere in Savannah. Mary Sue might be able to tell you where since she worked for Grace. Jasmine works at one of the tourist shops downtown, I think its Pirate's Treasure. I'm sorry I can't be of any more help." She let the water out of the sink, rinsed her hands, and dried them with a dishtowel.

"You've been a tremendous help."

"I'd do anything to support Laura. She's been really good to me. I feel so blessed to be working here with her instead of Grace. I've always felt sorry for poor Edna. Stuck with that …. Well I'd better not say what I was thinking."

Before she could finish, Nana barged in the kitchen like a whirlwind. "There you are. I thought you'd left without me. Who are we going to interview first?"

"Uh, Nana." I looked to Dee Dee for some help, but she had started helping Louise re-shelve the dried dishes.

"I think we'll try to find Mary Sue Bartlett first. Are you ready to go?"

"I sure am. Let's go!"

I was so shaken up with what Louise may have been about to explain, I hadn't noticed, but I had to admit, she looked very cute. Dressed in a dark blue jogging suit with a light blue tee shirt, she wore a matching blue baseball cap. Wearing a matching cap was something she'd recently started. I can truthfully say there was never a dull moment with Nana around.

"Let's tell Mama we're going."

Nana scooted out of the kitchen faster than a greased pig.

"Are you really going to let her go?" Dee Dee whispered.

"I guess so. I just couldn't tell her no. Anyway, Mama needs a break." We thanked Louise for her help and went to find Nana. We discovered her excitedly telling Mama about our sleuthing.

"Now don't you worry, Betty Jo. I'll keep an eye on the girls. I won't let them do anything stupid." This coming from the lady who on a whim decided to get a tattoo that would last a lifetime – well as much time as Nana had left.

"Trixie, thank you for letting Nana go along. I'd like to spend some time with Laura today. She needs all the support she can get."

I hugged Mama as tight as I could. I loved her so much. I realized I needed to spend some time alone with Mama. I wanted to share my feelings with her about Beau's proposal.

Dee Dee walked up. "Group hug?" We hugged and we laughed and we cried. The events of the past few days had taken its toll on all of us. *Lord, please don't let us wind up in the home for the bewildered before this is over.*

CHAPTER TWENTY-ONE

We piled in my car. It still harbored the new car smell. Dee Dee sat in the back and Nana rode shotgun. We decided to interview Jasmine first and save Mary Sue until lunch time. We drove down Jones Avenue, and headed toward the pier and pavilion. City officials had cordoned off the downtown area due to the arts and crafts festival. I hoped the walk to Pirate's Treasure wasn't too far and then recalled the physical therapist said moderate exercise would be good for my new knee.

Nana hopped out of the car before it completely stopped. I slammed the gearshift in park and followed her as fast as my gimpy leg would allow. *I could sure use some of her energy, Lord.*

"Come on girls. If you're waiting on me you're backing up," Nana cackled.

"Remember, I've got a new knee, Nana." Even though I now walked without a cane, I wasn't up to running marathons.

Tourists of every size and shape poked through booths filled with homemade items. Parents, accompanied by children begging for souvenirs, weaved their way through the throng of people. Couples held hands and made goo-goo eyes at each other. Images of Beau flashed in my mind. The void that filled my heart surprised me. I vowed to call Beau as soon as I had some alone time.

A shoulder shake from Dee Dee interrupted my thoughts. "Trix. Are you in there?"

"Sorry, I was in another world."

"The one where Beau lives?" At times she knew me better than I knew myself. It was *wonderful* to have Dee Dee along on this roller coaster ride better known as life. Her faith was a beacon for me in the storm I'd been riding the past couple of years.

We stopped at a few of the booths along the way. "Look at this picture frame with a sea shell border. Wouldn't it be perfect for a picture of me and George?" Nana turned around and shoved it in my face. I gave her a smile, but I still wasn't convinced George was on the up and up. I'd tell Beau what little information I'd gleaned.

I stopped a young man in costume and asked where the Pirate's Treasure was located. "Arrrrg, matey. It be located around the next corner." He bowed at his waist as he made a wide sweeping motion with his hat. I thanked him and we ventured on. He resembled Johnny Depp in *Pirates of the Caribbean. Lucky man.*

"Well, wasn't he the handsome one?"

When did Nana *not* think a man was handsome?

Dee Dee didn't miss a beat. "So Nana, you're a real pushover for the bad boy type?"

"Yep. I've been seeing George, you know." My head shot up. I wondered if she knew something we didn't. I gave Dee Dee a look to see if she caught Nana's reference. She raised her eyebrows in acknowledgement. We had to talk later.

We stopped in front of Pirate's Treasure. Beach-going necessities filled the display windows. Colorful tops and shorts, flip flops, children's sand toys, and even a striped beach umbrella decorated the outside area.

"Let's go in." Dee Dee pushed the door open and a bell tinkled overhead.

A gum smacking young girl in her teens greeted us. "May I help you?"

"Yes. Is Jasmine working today?"

"Sure. Want me to get her?" She tucked her hair behind her ear and exposed a row of earrings all the way up the side. *Ouch, that must've hurt.*

"Of course we do, dear." Nana wasn't one for beating around the bush.

"Nana. Be nice." A sense of dread filled me and I wished I'd left Nana with Mama.

"Watch it, Missy. Remember, I changed your diapers." Why did I always have the urge to roll my eyes when I was around Nana?

We looked around at the variety of merchandise. You could find anything you needed for a day or a week on the beach at Pirate's Treasure – an apt name.

"I'm Jasmine. How may I help you?" I turned around and faced an attractive woman. Her silky hair flowed to her waist. Even though it was obvious she was middle aged, her dark hair was absent of any gray. She wore little, if any, makeup. She had paired her white peasant blouse with a teal blue skirt that reached her ankles. A silver toe ring winked up at me. I could imagine others labeled her as an "old hippie" but I liked her style at once.

"Hi, Jasmine. I'm Trixie Montgomery and I write for *Georgia by the Way*, a magazine featuring the past and present stories of Georgia. Uh, I'm writing about the sea turtles and I'd like to interview you." I crossed my fingers and hoped she still had some involvement with the turtles.

"Well, I have a break coming up. Let me tell my manager, and then I'll be free for about fifteen or twenty minutes. Would that be long enough?"

"Sure. That'll be great." I looked at Dee Dee and smiled. She smiled back. Nana, engrossed in looking at the merchandise, was oblivious to our silent conversation. Jasmine disappeared through a door behind the register.

Dee Dee grabbed my arm and whispered in my ear. "You did it girl. She thinks you really work for a magazine."

"Dee Dee, I do work for a magazine."

"Oh yeah, that's right. You do." I wondered about Dee Dee at times. And this was one of them. Before I could question her sanity she put my mind at ease. "Aw, I was just pulling your leg, Trixie. You need to lighten up."

"I'm on my last nerve and you just stepped on it." I stuck out my bottom lip.

"I'm sorry, Trixie. I only wanted to see you laugh. I didn't mean to make you feel bad." She put her arm around my shoulder and squeezed. "You know I'm here for you. You don't have to face this alone. Your mom doesn't realize how draining it can be to gather and interview suspects. Right now she's thinking of helping her friend. She believes in you."

"I'm sorry, too. It's not only the murder that has me so upset."

"I know. Trixie, remember to pray about it. I believe the answer to Beau's proposal will come to you and when it does a peace will follow."

"Thanks, Dee Dee. I needed that little pep talk. Hey, where is Nana?"

"She was here just a minute ago. I wouldn't worry. She can't get into too much trouble in the store." Was she ever wrong.

Jasmine walked up, accompanied by a middle-aged man. "Trixie. This is Joe, my manager. I told him you worked for *Georgia by the Way* and he wanted to meet you." He stuck out his hand and I reached to shake it.

He drew back his hand as if he'd been bitten by a snake. His eyes bulged and his face turned a bright shade of red. He gasped for breath. I turned to Jasmine for help.

I was surprised to discover her face mirrored his. She'd be of no help to anyone. They stared over my shoulder and I turned to see what had caused such a reaction. I knew, without a doubt, the unbelievable image my eyes beheld would be etched in my mind forever.

CHAPTER TWENTY-TWO

Walking toward us was an apparition – no, on second glance I realized the vision was real. *Lord, please beam me up and transport me anywhere else.* Dressed in a skimpy, hot pink, two-piece bathing suit, with matching flip-flops, mimicking the high-stepping gait of a beauty queen, Nana glided toward us. An invisible hand squeezed the breath out of me and now I, too, gasped for air. The only one who retained the ability to speak was Dee Dee.

"Nana, what have you been up to?" Dee Dee grabbed a beach towel and wrapped it around Nana's shoulders. Nana pushed the covering away.

She placed a hand on her hip and twirled about. "How do I look?" We sputtered and coughed, unable to find words to describe her. "I found this cute bathing suit and knew hot pink would look great on me. And it's half-price – icing on the cake. Just wait till George sees me. His eyes will pop out of his head."

Well, she had that right. His eyes would probably never be the same. I knew mine wouldn't. When I spoke, my words squeaked out.

"Nana. For heaven's sake, go back to the dressing room. Dee Dee can help you while I talk to Jasmine." My ears felt like they were on fire. Why, oh why, didn't I leave Nana with Mama?

"Look, Missy." This was Nana's favorite name for me when she was upset. "Just because I have a little age on me doesn't mean you have to treat me like a doddering old fool." I wasn't so sure about the "old fool" part.

Still in shock, I would be forever beholden to Dee Dee for taking control of the situation. "Come on, Nana. Let's go see if we can find a cute sun dress to wear over your new suit." She grabbed Nana's arm and with the determination of an army general, she led Nana away.

I turned to Jasmine and her boss. My addled brain tried to come up with a plausible explanation for Nana's behavior. Before I could utter intelligent words, Joe said he had work to do and hurried away.

"I'm sorry, Jasmine. My great-aunt displays quirky behavior at times. My mama thinks she has the beginning of dementia, but I think she does it on purpose. The truth is probably somewhere in-between."

"Don't worry. Every family has a colorful character – mine was my grandfather." She reached over and straightened the pile of towels Dee Dee had toppled when she grabbed one to cover up Nana.

"Is there somewhere quiet we can talk?" I really just needed to sit down. The shock of seeing Nana half naked had left me weak in the knees.

"Sure. Let's go to the break room." I followed her through a maze of merchandise. We entered through a door labeled "Employees Only" where a lone table stood in the middle of the small room. A microwave sat on a counter, along with a coffee maker, and a variety of condiments. She pulled out a chair and sat down across from me. "Are you all right?"

"I'll be fine."

"Did you want to ask me some questions about the sea turtles?" She grabbed a Styrofoam cup and poured me a drink at a small sink. "You look a little pale."

I put the image of Nana in the back of my mind and focused on the task at hand. I sipped the cool water, then pulled notebook and pen from my bag, beginning with some general questions concerning the habits of mother and baby terrapins. It seemed no time at all when Jasmine checked the time on the microwave.

"I only have a few minutes left before my break's over." I knew I had to ask the hard questions before she left.

"Edna, the housekeeper at Ocean View Inn, told us you ran against

Grace for president of the local chapter of Save the Turtles." Jasmine's dark skin turned a shade lighter.

Her stare dared me to continue. I wondered if I gazed into the eyes of a murderer.

"She told us Grace used underhanded means to knock you out of the running and win over the board. The members heard you threaten Grace at one of the meetings."

"Why are you bringing all this up? It doesn't have anything to do with my concern for the sea turtles. It certainly doesn't have any business in your magazine."

"You're right. I do write for *Georgia by the Way* and I am writing an article, but I'm also here as a friend to Laura. Actually, she's my mama's friend, but I'm interviewing some of the people Grace had run-ins with."

Jasmine emitted an incredulous laugh. "You'll be here a long time, because you'll have to interview half the town." She scooted back her chair.

"Please." This wasn't going as planned. "Jasmine, I want to help Laura. Detective Baker's questioned her several times and she's worried the detective's placed her on the top of the suspect list."

She slowly sat back down and leaned her arms on the table.

A faraway look clouded her eyes and her fists clenched into balls. "Just thinking about that lady makes my blood boil. I moved here to make a fresh start and help with the sea turtles. It would have been a win–win situation for me. Up until I threw my hat in the ring to run for president, my life had changed for the better." She stopped for a minute, lost in her own thoughts. When she spoke, her voice possessed a hard edge.

"After that witch aired my past to the board and the members of the club, my life went from good to bad. The club didn't throw me out, but the members treated me differently. Sure, they were civil, but nobody was knocking down my door to be best friends. If it weren't for Joe giving me a chance, I don't know if I would even have a job."

She drew in a deep breath and looked me in the eye. "I'd like to say I'm sorry she's dead. But I can't." The list of people who wouldn't miss Grace continued to grow. I had one more question for Jasmine. I charged ahead like Sherman leading his march to the sea.

"Jasmine. Before you leave could you tell me where you were the night of Grace's murder?"

"Even though it's none of your business – I was in bed asleep. Now I've got to get back to work." This time she slid her chair back, ending the discussion with finality and headed toward the door. She reached for the handle when a knock on the door stopped her hand mid-air.

CHAPTER TWENTY-THREE

Hello. Anybody in there?" Nana's voice blasted through.

"Oh, no." I looked around, scouting for an avenue of escape. There wasn't one.

Jasmine opened the door. "We're finished. Come on in." She stepped back. Nana entered with Dee Dee on her heels. Jasmine made her escape past them.

"Thanks for your time." I spoke to her back, but doubted she even heard me.

Nana wore the jogging suit she'd worn this morning. I breathed a sigh of relief. I was amazed how Dee Dee could tame Nana, and winked at her. *Thank you, my friend.*

"Well, what did she confess, Trix?" Nana came over and stood beside me.

Dee Dee pulled out a chair. "How did it go?" Dee Dee thumbed toward the door.

"She didn't confess, but Grace is definitely not on Jasmine's 'A' list. She harbors a lot of anger toward Grace for bringing up her past to the club members. We need to keep her as a possible suspect." My stomach produced a noise akin to a small volcano. Nana and Dee Dee laughed.

"Somebody's hungry. Let's go find some lunch," Dee Dee jumped up.

"Best idea I've heard all day." I grabbed Nana's elbow and steered toward the exit. I didn't want her sidetracked by shiny do-dads on the way out. She'd wreaked enough havoc on this trip for a lifetime. Little was I to know she wasn't through.

We returned to the car without any major catastrophes. Dee Dee read the directions as we navigated down Jones Street. I turned on a side road to reach the Dari Delight where Mary Sue Bartlett worked. The block building needed some tender loving care. A few cars were scattered around the parking lot, but not as many as you'd expect at lunch time.

A bell hanging above the door tinkled to announce our arrival. Several voices hollered in unison for us to take a seat. We chose a table by the window. I grabbed the menus, stuck between the salt and pepper shakers and the napkin holder, and passed them out. I pulled a napkin from the container and wiped grease from the front of the plastic cover.

A middle-aged lady with a pencil stuck behind her ear, and dressed in black slacks and a once-white blouse, approached our table. "What can I get cha'?" She pulled a pencil from her ear and stuck her tongue to the lead. *Ugh.*

"Hi. We're looking for Mary Sue," Dee Dee said.

"Well, y'all came to the right place. You're lookin' at her." Drooped shoulders and hooded eyes surprised me to no end. Was this the same lady who'd hosted her own cooking show? "What can I do for ya?"

My stomach chose that moment to growl like a half- starved lion. "We'd like to order something to eat first." Dee Dee and I ordered the burger basket with french fries and onion rings. Nana ordered two hot dogs all the way, french fries, and a side of slaw. Then she inquired about dessert. Dee Dee shot me a look that said, "Where is she going to put all that food?" I shrugged.

"Okay, ladies. I'll put your order in and bring out your drinks." She hurried off toward the kitchen.

We continued our discussion about Jasmine and her interview while we waited on our food. "Dee Dee, grab the list and let's go over who we've talked to and who we have left to question." She reached in her gigantean bag and magically pulled out the notebook. She laid it on the table between us.

"Here ya' go. Two burger baskets and two dogs all the way." Mary Sue plopped the plates down in front of us. She reached in her pocket, brought out a bottle of ketchup, and placed it on the table. Dried goo clung to the sides. "Let me know if you need anything else."

I leaned my head in toward Nana and Dee Dee. "When she comes back for dessert we need some excuse to get her to sit down and talk with us."

Dee Dee rubbed her chin. "Hmm. Let me think."

"Just tell her the truth. Explain to her we're trying to help Laura and does she have any information she can share with us. We don't have to tell her more than that." Nana pulled the tablet closer and studied the names.

"That might work, Nana. Now, let's see who we've talked to so far. Dee Dee, call off a names."

Dee Dee scooted the pad back her way. "First, we talked to Edna, Grace's cook and housekeeper." She took a bite of her hamburger. Ketchup oozed off the bun and plopped on her plate.

"It's obvious no love was lost between those two. Edna felt trapped and murder might have seemed her only choice out of a terrible situation." For the next few minutes, quiet surrounded the table while we ate. I surveyed the dining area and noticed only a few diners. Maybe Mary Sue wouldn't be too busy to stop and talk.

Nana talked around a mouthful of hotdog. "Who's next?"

Dee Dee glanced at the notebook. "Louise. She didn't have a personal vendetta against Grace, but she's good friends with Edna. Unknowingly, she corroborated everything Edna said."

"I don't get the feeling Louise had anything to do with it. I can't say the same for Edna." We snagged bites in between our discussion. Dee Dee pointed to her mouth then to mine. I swiped the area with my napkin. I'd wiped a blob of ketchup off my face.

"Don't forget Ellie. Remember her reaction when you mentioned her meeting with John Porter on the beach? She was madder than a bull eyeing red." Dee Dee took an onion ring, slipped it on her finger and twirled it around like a hula-hoop. Laughter floated around the table.

"That's right. It's mighty suspicious my question solicited such a reaction. Let's keep her on the suspect list until we find out more about her."

"Is that all?"

"What about Jasmine? You just talked to her." Nana had made her hot dogs disappear quicker than a crab could burrow in the sand. She worked on digging the last little bit of slaw out of the container.

"Of course. Thanks, Nana. Jasmine needs to be on the list right beside Edna. Both of those ladies were wronged by Grace, and neither one of them showed any sorrow at her death."

"We still have several others to interview: Grace's husband Bert, the Daniels, Bubba Maxwell, the Sandersons and finally John Porter." Mary Sue walked up to the table and Dee Dee shoved the notebook back in her bag.

"You ladies need any refills? How about dessert?" She stacked a few of the dirty dishes and gathered a handful to carry with her.

I looked at the girls. "Banana pudding all the way around?" They nodded their agreement.

"Coffee with that?" We nodded in unison. "Okie dokie. I'll be right back."

We chatted while she rounded up our desserts. I hoped when she returned I'd be able to convince her to sit with us for a while. Only one other booth held customers. Laden with pudding and coffee, she approached our table.

"Here, let me help." I handed the bowls to Nana and Dee Dee and she served the coffee. I scooted over. "Please sit with us a minute."

She surveyed her surroundings. "I probably shouldn't, but I'll sit for just a few minutes." She eased down beside me and I heard a sigh. "Feels good to sit; my feet are killing me. Now, what are you ladies up to?"

Her blunt question startled me and I struggled to say something to lighten the mood.

"We want to know if you killed Grace Watkins." Nana blurted before I could speak. "Where were you Monday night?"

CHAPTER TWENTY-FOUR

My eyes rolled heavenward. *Lord please bless me with a healthy heaping of patience.* Although, I knew the way to learn patience was to handle more trials and wondered if it was too late to take back my prayer.

Dee Dee covered her mouth and faked a cough. I tried to follow up with damage control. "What she means is we're helping Laura. Detective Baker's questioned her several times and shows no interest in looking for other suspects. My Mama is good friends with Laura and she's asked me to help. Is there any information you can offer that would help us?"

"What makes you think I have anything to say about Grace?" She took a pinch of spilled salt and threw the grains over her left shoulder.

Dee Dee spoke up. "Edna, over at Ocean View Inn, told us how Grace maligned you."

Mary Sue's eyes widened and her tanned skin lost a little of its color. "Edna spoke out of turn. I don't know what you ladies are up to, but I don't have anything to say. Now if you don't mind, I need to get back to work." She stood up, ready to leave. I grasped her arm and gently tugged.

"Mary Sue, please. Grace tormented Laura, but we know she wasn't the only one targeted. What if Detective Baker focused his investigation on you and you knew you didn't do it. Would you want our help then?" Through her eyes, I glimpsed the wheels of thought spinning. She sat back down. I heaved a sigh of relief.

"You're right. I guess I was a little hasty, but I didn't want to get involved where Grace Watkins is concerned. That woman destroyed any trust I had in humankind."

My heart went out to Mary Sue. Even though my situation was different, the feeling of betrayal was the same. Thoughts of her pain brought back my own hurtful memories. Wade decided to present me with the surprise of my life. After years of marriage, he had approached me with his bags packed and told me he'd found his soul mate on the internet.

My world shattered that day as did my trust in others. My very identity was wrapped up in my beliefs as I knew them. Wade not only left me emotionally empty, but left our bank accounts depleted, as well. I should have felt vindicated when Wade slithered back into my life. He soon discovered his beautiful, blonde soul mate was a three hundred pound hussy who conned men for money. I didn't. After he returned home he rushed right into the arms of another woman.

Beau, my boyfriend, along with Dee Dee, worked wonders to restore my faith in people. I came to terms that humans were fallible and would disappointment us from time to time. But the most important thing I had learned is there is someone who loves us unconditionally and will never let us down.

"Earth to Trixie." Dee Dee reached across the table and shook my arm.

I composed myself and turned to Mary Sue. "Anything you can tell us about Grace will be appreciated."

"Hmm, where to start?" She stared at the ceiling as if all the answers floated in the air. "I remember when I came to Ocean View to work. I'd been through a nasty divorce and had a young daughter to care for. I was so excited to land a position in one of the most popular bed and breakfasts on the island."

I looked at Nana and Dee Dee sitting across from me. They shoveled in banana pudding as fast as they could. I understood why. This might not be the most pleasant looking diner, but they sure knew how to make dessert. I nibbled a spoonful as Mary Sue continued.

"She had us fill out a contract. I didn't pay much attention to the stack of papers as she shoved them in front of me to sign. At the time, I was so excited to have a job I'd have just about signed anything." She took a cloth tucked in her apron and wiped the table off. "I still regret that decision."

Nana with her usual lack of decorum asked, "Why? What was in them?"

Mary Sue's eyes went wide. "I'm gettin' there." She picked at a thumbnail. "The job worked out fine for a couple of years. I got to be good friends with Edna. We had a lot in common and we both loved to cook. I took Grace's recipes, which were all right but kind of bland and old-school, and doctored them up a little with my ideas to bring them into the current trends. You know, I came up with some gluten-free options, and I used some modern spices and ingredients with others." She sat up straighter. "It was my idea to begin using truffle oil in some of the fancier dishes."

We all studied our empty pudding bowls.

"Word spread and some of the locals came just to eat one of my meals," she continued. "But instead of giving me credit for the recipes, she claimed anything I added was hers according to that contract I'd signed. She threatened to sue me if I made a fuss." She looked around the table. "Grace fought me on a lot of the changes, but she had to admit we were finally on the map." She glanced at our empty bowls. "Seconds?"

So that was why the two women fought like two parakeets in a pillowcase. Jealousy.

"No."

"Yes." I guess two yes's outweigh a no anytime.

"Won't take but a minute. I think I'll take an official break and drink a cup of coffee with you." She jumped up quicker than a grasshopper.

"Trixie, look and see if I have anything between my teeth." Dee Dee furnished me a Whitney Houston smile. I inspected her pearly whites for any stray food particles.

"There's a speck of black pepper right in front."

She dug at it with a nail. "Oh no. Mr. Right might walk inside any minute and mistake it for a rotten tooth." She rumbled around in her bag and came up with a mirror. "Yikes." She rummaged around a little more and withdrew a small case of dental floss.

"You're not going to do what I think you're going to do, are you?"

"There's nobody at this table but us. Just remember, what happens at this table stays at this table." Her golden laughter filled the air.

Nana contributed to the fun. "What happens on the island stays on the island." By the time Mary Sue returned to the table with a new round of pudding and a fresh pot of coffee we were laughing like a pack of hyenas.

She sat the food on the table and gave us a disapproving look. "You ladies don't sound like you're too upset about Laura's troubles."

CHAPTER TWENTY-FIVE

Mary Sue sank down beside me. Her stern look put the kibosh on our laughter.

"Sorry. You know what they say, 'laughter is the best medicine.'"

"Yeah, I guess so." She doctored her coffee and took a long drink. "Mmm. That's good, even if I did make it." Three heads bobbed in agreement. Images of Nana's head atop a bobblehead doll invaded my thoughts.

Dee Dee leaned forward, silently willing Mary Sue to continue.

"Well, like I was saying. We'd built up a loyal following of locals at the bed and breakfast. Then one day, a friend of mine, Deidra, got a promotion and knew about my frustration, asked me to work for her in one of the beachside restaurants, The Blue Dolphin. The pay was double what I made at Ocean View and she was going to give me full credit for the dishes. I couldn't turn it down. I knew this would be a great chance to make things better for me and my daughter."

An elderly couple walked in the door and Mary Sue hollered, "Have a seat." She stood up, but one of the other waitresses gave her a wave to say 'I've got it.' She sat back down.

"Mary Sue, what happened after you left Ocean View?" Nana and Dee Dee had wolfed down their second helping of banana pudding and now sipped on their coffee. A few bites remained in the bottom of my bowl.

Dee Dee eyed my pudding with genuine longing. "Are you going to finish that?"

"Yes, I am. If you cherish your fingers, don't even think about reaching over here." I scooted the bowl closer for protection. Mary Sue looked from me to Dee Dee and back to me. I'm sure she thought we'd escaped from the home for the bewildered.

She shook her head and smiled. "Y'all have a unique relationship don't you?" We nodded in agreement. I'm not sure what she meant by unique, but I assumed she meant 'special.' "I wish I still had a best friend." She stared into the distance, possibly remembering a time when she did.

"Scoot out of the way, Dee Dee. I need to go to the little ladies room." Nana gave Dee Dee's arm a little shove – as if her petite frame could move Dee Dee an inch.

"Sure thing, Nana."

"Dee Dee, why don't you go with Nana?" I gave her an exaggerated wink. I thought she could keep an eye on Nana and give us a few minutes to talk. Dee Dee missed my hint.

"I don't need to go. Isn't it wonderful?" In the past, Dee Dee couldn't go an hour without having to tinkle. The new patches were nothing short of a miracle, but this was one time I needed her to go.

"Are you having that eye problem again, Trix?"

"No, I'm not. Are you sure you don't need to go?" I winked again. This time she received my telepathic message.

"Come on, Nana." She and Nana headed to the ladies' room giggling like two teenagers.

"You're blessed to have your grandmother around."

"She's my great-aunt. And yes, I'm blessed." I looked upward. *Please help me to remember how blessed I am.* Sometimes life got in the way and stole the awareness of our blessings. This was something I needed to work on.

"Where were we? My train of thought derailed." She laughed a little too loud at her own wit. A sure sign of tattered nerves.

"You were saying what happened to you when you left Ocean View."

I prompted, scraping the bottom of the bowl for another dab of that delicious pudding.

"Everything was great for a while. Deidra featured my dishes in the menu of her restaurant. Before long, the customers followed us over, and their traffic doubled." Mary Sue refilled our coffee cups.

"We have a little television station that broadcasts local news and activities. Deidra wanted to get the word out about The Blue Dolphin, so she pitched the idea of a cooking show from our kitchen. They took her up on it."

"Edna told us you hosted your own show."

"It wasn't long before I was a local celebrity. People recognized me right off and would ask me about my recipes. Between working on the show and at the restaurant, I made pretty good money. For once, I didn't have to worry about paying bills. It was nice."

I could relate to Mary Sue. When Wade left, there were many nights I laid awake wondering how I'd make it through the next month. It took a while before I bounced back on my feet.

Nana and Dee Dee sidled up to the table. "All done," Nana announced. "What did we miss?"

"Mary Sue was just telling me about her cooking show."

Nana leaned forward. "We heard Grace ruined that for ya." So much for tact. I was worried how Mary Sue would react to Nana's bluntness, but she calmly eyed Nana.

"You're right, Nana. Grace ruined everything." She sighed and rested her chin in her hands like someone resigned to disappointment. "She watched the show and claimed I'd used her recipes as the base for my dishes. She said the contract prohibited me from using them anyplace else but her restaurant. Some of them did have the same basic ingredients, and I changed them around, but that didn't matter to Grace." Mary Sue held up the coffee pot for a refill – we declined with a shake of our heads.

"What did Grace do?" Dee Dee stacked the bowls and shoved them to the side.

"She went crazy, that's what she did." Green eyes full of fire replaced the defeated look Mary Sue wore just minutes before. "She got herself a lawyer and stalked me everywhere I went, she even came to the show and disrupted taping. The studio got scared of a lawsuit and started looking for my replacement. Scared to death I'd never find another job, I quit The Blue Dolphin and lost the show, too. They wouldn't even keep me on as a stage hand." Her face flushed a deep pink. "Some of the kids at school even picked on my Sarah Joe. We were about to move away but it all settled down."

I laid my hand on her arm. "I'm sorry, Mary Sue. It seems Grace spread her malice from one end of the island to the other. She had to be one unhappy person to feel the need to lash out at others." Thoughts of how miserable she must have been almost made me feel sorry for her. Then I remembered all the people she'd hurt.

"Yeah." Deep in thought, she visited a place we couldn't follow. Then she spoke slowly and deliberately. "It was just a matter of time before someone put a stop to her meanness."

CHAPTER TWENTY-SIX

Looks like death decided it was time to knock on her door," Nana said.

"Or somebody determined that for her." I looked at Mary Sue and tried to imagine a killer. I failed to picture her as a murderer. But I'd learned the hard way that even the gentlest of humans could become angry over wrongs done to them and their families, and then justify retaliation. Everyone will face this challenge in life and ultimately have to make a choice on how to react. Thankfully, most people rise to the challenge and realize the hard knocks of life can make you stronger.

Dee Dee reached across the table and jiggled my arm. "Trixie! You're staring."

"Oh, my goodness. I'm so sorry. I took a trip and lost my way back." I laughed, praying Dee Dee and Nana would join me. Their laughter was music to my ears. Even Mary Sue was gracious enough to laugh with me.

"Ladies, it's time for me to go back to work. I can't imagine how my sad story can be of any use to you, but I hope it helps Laura in some way."

I covered her hand with mine. "Thank you. I'm sure it wasn't easy dredging up old memories." Her doleful eyes reflected the pain in her soul. I was familiar with the agonizing hurt remembrances could trigger. All I had to do was conjure up thoughts of Wade.

I was thankful, through Dee Dee's companionship and her strong faith, I'd learned to let go of some of the past hurts. Friendship like ours was as sweet as the nectar of a honeysuckle on a summer's day.

The bell on the door tinkled and Mary Sue yelled "have a seat," breaking the mood. She grabbed a handful of dishes and left to return to a job Grace had forced her to take. Could the reminder day after day of what she had lost, of the added anguish of her child's pain, drive her to seek revenge? I didn't know, but I intended to find out.

"I don't know about y'all, but I'm plum tuckered out. How about we go back to the bed and breakfast and rest up?" Dee Dee stood up and stretched.

"Sounds like a wonderful idea." My knee ached a little and the respite would bring sweet relief.

"Times a'wastin'. I think we should move on to the next person on the list." Nana was certainly a little fireball of energy. "And don't even think about rolling your eyes, Missy."

I wouldn't dare. "Nana, I wouldn't think of it." I linked my arm with hers as we walked to the car.

"Humph."

Dee Dee grabbed Nana's other arm and we strolled along like the three Musketeers.

As we drove away from town, we left the crowd behind and headed to Seaside Cottage. I looked forward to a breather. Afterwards, Dee Dee and I could get together and regroup. Tomorrow we could drive to Savannah and interview Grace's ex-husband, Bert, and get back in time to attend the Pirate Fest. And I wanted – no, needed – to call Beau. I realized how much I missed him.

"Do you think Laura would mind if George came over and ate with us tonight?" Nana had fallen head over heels for George. He was nice enough, but I wasn't convinced he was on the up and up. If he came over tonight, I could pick his brain and maybe find out some personal information about him.

"I'm sure she won't mind," Dee Dee assured Nana. "Okay, who blocked the driveway with their Crown Vic?"

"Oh, no. That's Detective Baker's car. It can't be a good sign he keeps showing up at Laura's." I pulled in behind him and parked.

When we entered, tension as thick as pea soup filled the room. Detective Baker and one of his cronies occupied the couch. Mama and Laura claimed the two wing back chairs. A coffee table laden with desserts and drinks sat between them. Laura, ever the gracious hostess, had made sure her nemesis was well cared for.

"Trixie, I'm so glad you're back. Detective Baker's been waiting to talk to you."

"Me?" Suddenly, my knee throbbed. I plopped in the nearest chair.

"Yes, Ms. Montgomery." He scooted to the edge of the couch, leaned forward with elbows on knees, and regaled me with his full attention. "It's been brought to my attention you've been questioning some of the locals."

"Yeah. Isn't it great how she uses her work as an excuse to interview suspects?" Nana spoke between bites as she made her point by shaking a potato chip at the detective.

God please beam me up. How could I love Nana so much and feel like killing her at the same time? "What Nana means is I've been interviewing people for my article on Savannah and Tybee Island and they just happen to know Grace. What a coincidence."

"Yes, what a coincidence," Detective Baker said in a mocking tone. Somehow I didn't think he believed me.

Nana wouldn't shut up. "That's not what I meant at all. Trixie's helped solve two murders and I'm sure she'll be able to help you crack this one."

Detective Baker's face turned bright red. "Ma'am, I don't need any help."

Dee Dee jumped up and grabbed Nana by the elbow. "Nana, I need you to help me for a minute." I shot her a grateful look. She gently pulled Nana up and escorted her toward the door.

"What do you need help with? I'm not through eating." I could hear Nana grousing all the way down the hallway. I owed Dee Dee.

Laura sat with her mouth agape, and Mama shook her head. I could have sworn I saw a hint of a smile appear on the Detective's partner. I should be used to Nana's antics by now, but I had a terrible urge to pull up a rug and slink under it like a snake going into its hidey-hole.

The Detective managed to speak. "Ms. Montgomery, your reputation precedes you. I know you have a habit of sticking your nose into matters that are none of your business. I have no intention of letting you railroad this investigation. Do you understand?"

"Uh, yes sir, I do. But what about my job? I have to conduct interviews for my article." I held my breath. If I couldn't interview people, I'd never be able to help Laura.

etective Baker eyed me long and hard before he answered. "You can conduct your interviews, but I'd better not get another call that you're harassing people about this case."

I exhaled. "Okay." He didn't say I couldn't interview suspects. He just said it shouldn't get back to him. I would have to be more subtle. And keep Nana at bay. "Detective, while you're here, could you tell us if you've made any progress in finding who the killer is? I've gathered that Grace made a lot of enemies." I figured it wouldn't hurt to remind him other people besides Laura might have wanted to kill Grace.

"Ms. Montgomery, I'm well aware of Grace's personality, but Laura has a strike against her the others don't. Her fingerprints were all over the murder weapon. Now if you'll excuse me, I need to get back to work." Detective Baker and junior Detective Taylor left without a second look.

"I don't know what you wanted me for, Dee Dee," Nana said. She came in the room, Dee Dee trailing behind her. "You could have picked out what you wanted to wear without me. Oh well, I understand why you'd want my advice. I just don't understand why you needed me right when I was talkin' to the detective."

Dee Dee gave Nana a shoulder hug. "Thanks, Nana. That yellow and orange outfit will be the talk of the town." She looked at me. "Did the detective leave?"

"Yes, and I'm glad because I'm about to drop. Anyone ready for a nap?" Dee Dee was the only one who took me up on my offer. We headed upstairs and plopped down on our beds.

"Trixie, do you have any thoughts on who might have killed Grace?"

"I'm not sure, Dee. I figure when we finish interviewing everyone on our list we can go to Detective Baker and give him the information we've gathered. I know he's going to be mad we interfered, but I don't think there's anything else we can do. It's too dangerous to go after the killer, even if we have an idea who it might be."

"Yeah, I guess you're right. Have you decided on the big question yet?"

"What big question are you talking about?" Of course, I knew what she was talking about. I just wanted to pull her chain.

She grabbed a pillow and threw it at me. I felt a cool breeze as it whizzed by. "You know exactly what I mean."

"I know. I thought we could use a good laugh."

"You're right about that, but you're not going to make me forget my question."

"I haven't had much time to think about Beau with my focus on the murder investigation, but it's been in a corner of my mind. Maybe I'm afraid to consider it. Dee Dee, he's so good to me and he's such a good Christian man. With that combination you would think I couldn't go wrong. I don't know why I have this niggling feeling in the back of my mind: what if?"

Dee Dee came over and sat next to me. "Trix, you've been through a lot. I know it was hard on you when Wade up and left. Once you've been betrayed by the one person you think will protect you, it's hard to trust again. But Beau isn't Wade. There comes a time when you have to let go and let God."

"I know, Dee Dee. You're right; Beau is nothing like Wade. I know in my heart what the answer is. I've known since he asked me. It's just saying the words out loud. Oh well, in the words of Scarlett O'Hara, 'oh fiddle-dee-dee I'll think about this tomorrow.'" She squeezed my hand and returned to her bed. Before I knew it I heard soft snoring.

I turned toward the wall and tried to stop the thoughts that swirled in my head. Finally, sleep called my name. My dreams were more confusing than when I was awake. Grace ran along the beach holding a garden gnome yelling, "You killed me, you killed me!" Laura ran after Grace yelling, "I didn't do it. Give me back my gnome." Nana, dressed in a hot pink two-piece bathing suit, ran after Laura yelling, "Wait for me. I'll help you solve the murder." Last but not least, Dee Dee and I brought up the rear yelling and flailing our arms. I was unable to decipher what we said.

"Hey, wake up." I looked into the familiar face of Mama. "Were you running from someone? Your feet were churning the covers." Mama chuckled softly. It was good to hear her laugh. Even at my expense.

"Something like that." I stretched my arms above my head and emitted a loud yawn. "I must have been wiped out." I reached for my cell phone I'd placed on the bedside table. "What time is it? I haven't missed dinner have I?" My phone showed the time was a little before six.

"That's why I came up to get you. Everyone's gathered downstairs. George arrived a few minutes ago." Mama sat down beside me. "Trixie, I want to tell you how much I appreciate you and Dee Dee helping Laura. I felt so bad for her. I've known Laura for years and I feel strongly she couldn't have murdered Grace."

"Mama, I don't say it enough, but I appreciate all you've done for me. You lifted me up when I was lower than a snake's belly and helped me back on my feet. I love you." I could feel the tears pooling in the corners of my eyes.

"Aw, honey." She comforted me in a bear hug. "I love you, too." I noticed I wasn't the only one with teary eyes. "Come on; let's go get something to eat."

"Okay, let me freshen up and I'll be down in a minute." I didn't want to scare anyone with my porcupine hair. A few minutes later I descended the stairs. I looked around and noticed everyone was present. Dee Dee, Nana and George were at one table. Mama, Laura, and Ellie Sloan were at another. Harold and Cassie Daniels sat at another table.

Laura jumped up and headed toward the kitchen. "Now that we're all here I'll help Louise serve." Once again, Louise outdid herself. They placed the feast on a central table and everyone served their own plates. We dined on baked ham, slaw, potato salad, baked beans, green beans, and biscuits. We had a choice of peach cobbler or seven layer chocolate cake for dessert.

We sat around the table and talked between bites of delectable food. Nana recounted the events of the day to George. I didn't feel comfortable with her sharing information, but didn't know how to stop her without causing a scene.

The door to the kitchen opened and in scurried Captain Jack. Laura stood up and started toward the cat. "Oh Jack, what are you doing in here?" He scooted past her and ran under our table.

Dee Dee reached under the table and scooped him up. "Look! He has something in his mouth."

CHAPTER TWENTY-EIGHT

Dee Dee pulled out what appeared to be a piece of jewelry from Captain Jack's mouth. As it was covered with sand it was hard to tell. She took a cloth napkin and dipped it in a water glass. Each swipe revealed a little more of the treasure.

"May I?" George grabbed the piece from Dee Dee. His eyes widened. "Cartier pink gold with diamonds."

Those of us sitting around the table gaped. By this time the others in the room wondered what was happening. Laura voiced her query. "What is it?"

An animated Dee Dee spoke up. "It's a bracelet. Captain Jack's found a diamond bracelet." Everyone rushed over to take a look.

Harold Daniels let out a long whistle. "Look at those diamonds." He grabbed for the bracelet. "Finders keepers, right?" George drew his hand back a lot faster than I thought a man his age could move.

"Uh, I think this is something we need to call Detective Baker about. After all, Captain Jack was at the scene of the crime. This could be some kind of evidence. Does anyone recognize the bracelet?" Out of the corner of my eye I noticed Ellie leave the room. "I can hold onto it until the authorities arrive."

"No." *Well, that was to the point.* What was going on with him? "What I mean is, I will keep it safe until Detective Baker gets here."

Not wanting to start a scene, I let it go. I called the detective and relayed his message to the others. "He'll be here in about an hour and he wants everyone to be available when he arrives."

"Why don't I get Louise to make a fresh pot of coffee? We can leave the desserts out and you can help yourselves." Laura walked over to where I stood. "Do you think this might be evidence from Grace's murder?"

"I don't know, Laura, but Captain Jack was digging around Grace when I found her body. I remember him running away."

"I can't picture her owning a Cartier bracelet. She'd squeeze a nickel until it screamed." Laura lifted an eyebrow. "Why would she have it in her possession?"

"Good question. Maybe Detective Baker can check it out."

"I think I'll help Louise. Staying busy keeps my mind off things." She shook her head and wrinkled her brow. "I don't look forward to seeing him again." She walked over, whispered in Mama's ear, and then they headed for the kitchen.

I noticed Harold and Cassie Daniels sitting in the living room. This would be a good chance to talk with them. Dee Dee and Nana sampled the coffee and desserts. George had disappeared. I contemplated why he was so interested in the bracelet, but he wasn't about to share the reason with me. I intended to find out, though.

I poured a cup of java and sat down across from the Daniels. "This has been an interesting evening." I took a sip of the hot liquid and savored the flavor. It tasted delicious.

"Yeah. I told Cassie I didn't want to come to Tybee Island. And I sure didn't want to stay at a bed and breakfast." He said 'bed and breakfast' like it was a dirty word. "It's like staying with distant relatives that you hardly know. Now look what's happened. We're right smack dab in the middle of a murder investigation."

Cassie's face flushed. I'm sure her husband's little tirade embarrassed her. "Daniel, you don't have to be rude. I'm sure Trixie doesn't want to hear you whine." She took a sip and turned to me. "I'm sorry, dear. This has been hard on both of us. When Harold retired we thought we'd be able to find some peace and quiet through travel. It seems we've gotten just the opposite. It's terrible what happened to Grace, and even worse Laura seems to be the main suspect." She shook her head like she couldn't believe they'd landed in the middle of this mess.

"I'm trying to help Laura by asking everyone where they were Monday evening. Do you remember what you were doing?" I crossed my fingers they'd be willing to talk.

"What do you want us to do? Incriminate ourselves to get Laura off the hook?"

Cassie sucked in a breath. "Harold! Why are you being so rude? Trixie's just trying to help, and we don't have anything to hide." She turned toward me. "We went for a walk on the beach after we ate. Then we decided to go downtown and look around. We came home around ten and went to bed early. We were wiped out from the drive."

"You can ask that girl, Ellie. She was downtown, too, with that Porter fellow. Both of them saw us."

"Really? She was with John Porter?" This definitely put a twist on things. I felt stronger than ever she knew Porter before they arrived on Tybee Island. But why would they hide the fact they knew each other?

"That's what I said."

Cassie shrank into herself. I sensed her husband's brusqueness often embarrassed her.

We sat silent for a while eating cookies and sipping our coffee. The doorbell interrupted our muse. Laura slowly walked toward the door as if she were walking to a firing squad.

"Good evening." Detective Baker and his ever-present sidekick Detective Taylor entered the room. "I want to talk with everyone who was present when the bracelet was discovered."

I volunteered my assistance. "I'll be glad to round them up." It took a few minutes to find Dee Dee and Nana, who'd stepped outside for some fresh air. Everyone else was in the house. Except for George.

"Uh, I can't find George."

"Did someone say my name?" George walked up, dapper as ever. Not a worry line etched on his mature face.

"Could I see the bracelet in question?"

George reached into his pocket and slowly pulled out the now sparkling clean tennis bracelet. Oh my goodness. What did he do to make it look brand new? I had a hunch Detective Baker wasn't going to be happy with this. Why would George take the initiative to tamper with evidence? This brash decision added fuel to my suspicions of him.

The detective reached for the shiny bracelet. "Is this what it looked like when it was found?" He looked directly at me. "I thought you said it was covered with sand."

CHAPTER TWENTY-NINE

Detective, I take the blame for this." George didn't seem worried he'd destroyed evidence. "I'm somewhat of a jewelry connoisseur and when I saw this piece I couldn't help it. I cleaned the bracelet up to see if it really was a Cartier. It is."

Detective Baker stared at George as if he could see right through him. "Don't you know not to tamper with evidence from a crime?"

"I'm sorry, sir. But we don't really know it's evidence from a crime, do we?" George had a point, but it was too much of a coincidence for Captain Jack to be running from the scene with something shiny in his mouth.

He exchanged an exasperated look with his partner. "It's too late to do anything about your mistake now." He looked around the room and made eye contact with everyone present. "If you find anything else, *do not handle it*. Put it in a plastic bag and call me immediately. Is there anything about those instructions you don't understand?" Heads shook back and forth, accompanied by a chorus of "no."

"Ms. Montgomery, I'd like to consult with you in my office in the morning. I want to go over your statement concerning the crime scene. For the rest of you, don't leave the island. This is not over yet!" He turned so abruptly he almost bumped into Detective Taylor, who followed him like a baby duck following his mama.

When the front door closed on them for what I hoped was the last time that night, Laura spoke first. "I'm tired to the bone. I'm going to retire for the evening. Please treat this as your home. Louise will leave night-time snacks out for everyone. Good night, and I hope you have a restful sleep."

I walked over to where she stood by Mama. Laura looked like she could use more than a night of peaceful sleep. Her hair needed a good comb through and her rumpled clothes looked as if she'd slept in them. She was bare of make-up and her skin revealed a sickly pallor. The bags under her eyes reminded me of a woman who'd given up on life. Memories of when I had been at my lowest, after Wade left, flooded my mind. I had been so thankful for the help my friends and loved ones offered. How could I not do the same for Laura?

Mama hugged Laura. "You'll continue to be in my prayers. Let Trixie and Dee Dee do what they can and we'll leave the rest up to God."

"I want to believe everything will turn out all right, but it's hard to muster up faith when you're in the midst of the storm. I'm calling a lawyer tomorrow."

I took the opportunity to give Laura a hug. "I understand how you feel. I've been where you are." She gaped at me in disbelief. "Really? You've been accused of a murder?"

I couldn't help but chuckle. "Well, no. But I've been to the valley where it's hard to find strength. Your friends' faith can help strengthen your assurance. Before you know it, yours will be strong again." *Wow, did I just give Laura a pep talk about faith?*

It wasn't that long ago Dee Dee had given me the same pep talk. I was a firm believer a friend could be a good influence and help you through the hard times. Dee Dee and Beau had proven it over and over. Now it was my turn to share that faith with Laura. She offered me a weary and not-so-sure smile, but at least it was an attempt. *Dear Lord, please help me help Laura.*

She went on to bed while the rest of us milled around and waited to discover what Louise would bring out for a night-time snack. I'd never been on a cruise, but I imagined this was what it would be like where food was the favorite pastime of the tourists.

I spotted Ellie sitting in a corner. She held a mug of coffee. This would be a great chance to talk with her. The burning question was, did she know John Porter before they arrived on the island or not. I refilled my cup and wandered over to where she sat. I nonchalantly took a seat next to her.

"Hi." Great conversation starter.

She looked at me like I was a fly in her soup. "Hi."

"This has been a real bummer for our vacation. How about yours?"

"Yeah, a real bummer." Okay, this line of questioning wasn't getting me anywhere. I decided to pull out all the stops.

"Harold Daniels told me they ran into you and John Porter downtown the night of Grace's murder. Did you know John before you came to the island?" For a fleeting moment I detected a look in her eyes that said 'oh no.' But it was gone as quick as it came.

"Uh, no, I didn't know him. We ran into each other outside and decided it would be nice to go downtown for a while." She tilted her head and gave me a wary look. "Why do you want to know? I don't see where this is any of your business."

"I'm trying to help Laura and I can only do so by asking questions."

"Well, if I were you, I'd leave that to Detective Baker. One person has already turned up dead." The hair on my neck stood up. Was this a harbinger I'd later regret?

She stood up. "I've had a long day and if you don't mind, I'm going to bed." She didn't hang around for my permission.

I made my way over to a little group huddled together comprised of Mama, Dee Dee, Nana, and George. "I'm going up to my room to call Beau. This has been a stressful day and I could use someone to bounce ideas off of."

Nana gave me an exaggerated wink. "Sure honey, we understand. You go ahead and 'bounce' ideas off Beau." She turned to Dee Dee. "Why don't you come up to our room and keep me and Betty Jo company and give the lovebirds some privacy." Nana cackled. I loved that about Nana. She could make me smile even when I didn't feel like smiling. And I let myself enjoy thinking about Beau that way.

We bade the Daniels goodnight and moseyed up the stairs. Dee Dee came in and grabbed her pajamas. "I'll take my bath and visit with the girls while you're on the phone."

"I don't think I'll be that long, but I'll give you a holler when I'm done." I appreciated the private time with Beau.

CHAPTER THIRTY

H i, Babe." The sound of his voice sparked a longing. I knew without a doubt I wanted to share my life with him. Yes, there was that old niggling doubt that recurred, but I didn't want to lose out on a chance at happiness.

"Beau, it's so good to hear your voice." I ached to touch him, to hold his hand.

"It's good to hear you, too. How are things going on the island? Have you been able to get information on that George character?"

"He didn't give me an address, but I did get his tag number. I hope this helps. I know there's more to him than meets the eye. I'm afraid he's up to no good."

"Trix, I know you have a deep desire to help others and anything I say won't change that. But I want you to be careful and please give the information you gather to the detectives and let them do their jobs."

"We only have a couple more people to interview and then I'll hand the material over to Detective Baker. I'm not too concerned about the interviews; it's Nana who's going to be the death of me." A hearty laugh blasted through the phone. Beau loved Nana and he took her antics with a grain of salt. Of course, he didn't have to live with her. "Beau, it's not funny. Do you know she tried on a hot pink two-piece swimsuit and then modeled it for everyone in the store? I could have lifted the floor and crawled under it. If it hadn't been for Dee Dee's fast thinking I don't know what I would've done."

"Don't take it too seriously, hon. She won't be with you forever." I knew he was right.

"I know. I love her dearly, even if she makes me want to pull my hair out." I don't know how long we'd been talking when Dee Dee stuck her head in the door and whispered, "You about through?" I looked at the clock and realized we'd talked for forty-five minutes. I nodded my head. She gave a little wave and shut the door.

We said our good-byes and promised to talk the next day. As soon as we disconnected I missed him. I couldn't wait to get home and give him the answer he was patiently waiting to hear.

The bathroom door opened and Dee Dee peeked in. "Hey, can I come in now? I'm ready to hit the sack and read for a little while if I can keep my eyes open." Dee Dee came around the door dressed in a pair of red pajamas covered with white kittens. I couldn't remember a time when we'd spent the night together when she didn't have on kitty PJs. She was definitely devoted to her babies – I mean her cats.

"New pajamas?"

"Yeah. I bought them just for our trip." She plucked at the flannel fabric. "What do you think?"

I thought, *they kind of look like the rest of your pajamas*, but I said, "Nice." Her smile was worth the compliment.

We talked a little longer and Dee Dee snuggled in bed with her book. I turned over and willed my errant thoughts to focus on Beau and our future to replace the memories of murder and mayhem that tried to hold my mind hostage. I faded into sleep, dreaming of Beau's sweet kisses.

I awoke to Dee Dee singing, "Wake Up, You Sleepyhead!" I covered my head with my pillow, and she jerked it off.

"Oh no, you don't. We need to hurry if we're driving to Savannah this morning to interview Grace's ex. I want plenty of time to find some costumes for tonight's Pirate Fest."

"Please, let me sleep ten more minutes," I whined. She pulled off my covers.

"Nope. I'm already dressed. Come on, get up. I'm going downstairs to drink a cup of coffee. If you're not down in fifteen I'm coming for you."

I lobbed my pillow toward her, but missed my mark. Her laughter floated down the hall. To meet Dee Dee's time requirement I splashed my face with water and threw on a pair of jeans and tee shirt. I could come up later and put on my face.

We managed to convince Nana to stay with Mama. I suggested they find Nana a costume for the evening festivities and headed to Savannah.

On the drive over we discussed what we planned on wearing to the Pirate Festival. The choices for women were few. You could be a lady pirate, wench, or princess. We decided princess or lady pirate worked best for us.

We headed downtown to the Mercer Williams House where Bert, Grace's ex-husband, worked as a security guard. Dee Dee studied the brochure for directions. "Hey, listen to this.

The Mercer House was designed by New York architect John S. Norris for General Hugh W. Mercer, great-grandfather of Johnny Mercer. Construction of the house began in 1860, was interrupted by the Civil War, and was later completed, circa 1868, by the new owner, John Wilder.

"I knew Johnny Mercer was connected to the house, but I wasn't sure he ever lived there."

Dee Dee continued, "It goes on to say Jim Williams bought the house in 1969 and began a two year restoration." She lowered the brochure. "He's the guy who was portrayed in the movie, *Midnight in the Garden of Good and Evil.*

"I know. Wouldn't it make a great story for *Georgia by the Way*? I mentally filed information to use at a later date. "If we have time, I'd love to take the tour. Maybe take some pictures and buy a book or two for research." My interest piqued as she continued to read.

CHAPTER THIRTY-ONE

J im Williams, accused of murder, claimed self-defense. After four trials he was acquitted." Dee Dee finished reading from the brochure.

"I wonder how he warranted four trials. I'll put that on my research list. He definitely beat the bullet."

Dee Dee flipped the brochure over. "Listen to this. *Jim Williams was one of Savannah's earliest and most dedicated private restorationists. He began to restore houses in 1955 at the age of 24, the same year the Historic Savannah Foundation was founded. It was the beginning of a career that would span more than 30 years and result in saving over 50 houses in Savannah and the Lowcountry. When he bought the Mercer house in early 1969, it had been vacant almost a decade. Thus began a painstaking restoration that lasted two years and was finished in time for a Christmas party.*

"We're getting close. It should be in the next square." I knew from my research that Savannah boasted 22 squares. These squares, first designed by General James Oglethorpe, made this unique city a beautiful place to visit. I looked in awe at the huge oaks draped in Spanish moss standing like sentinels throughout the city. The traffic moved at a leisurely pace around the squares. Tour buses dotted the traffic.

"Look!" Dee Dee thrust the brochure in front of my face. "There it is. See? It's the same house as in the picture."

I slammed on the brakes, glanced in the rearview and breathed a sigh of relief. Thankfully, no cars were in sight. "Girl, what are you doing? Trying to get us killed?"

Dee Dee turned around to look, too. "Aw, Trix, you do tend to over-react. There isn't anyone behind us." She pointed at a two story, red brick house across the square. "Look at that. It takes up the whole block. Hurry and park; I can't wait to take the tour."

"Yikes, I haven't parallel parked in a coon's age." The secret was out when I scraped my tires on the curb during my third try. The driver in the waiting car honked their horn. I didn't blame them.

"I can tell," Dee Dee said.

"A perfect job. Thank you very much." I air pumped my fist.

"Yeah. And it only took four tries."

Dee Dee sure knew how to put a damper on a girl's accomplishment.

I grabbed my camera and clicked away. The Mercer Williams House stood proud among other historic homes in the area. Tall arched windows decorated the Italianate mansion. Ironwork balconies surrounded the stately windows. I took pictures from the front of the house and then from several different angles. I'd learned through my work that it took many shots to produce one or two images good enough to be print worthy.

We walked around to the back of the house where other tourists waited in line for tickets. A young lady informed everyone it would be twenty minutes before the next tour so we decided to browse around in the gift shop. I glimpsed through books showcasing the interior, making me even more anxious to see it for myself.

"Trix, here they come. I guess we're next." We stepped back to let the line of tourists pass by.

"Ladies and gentlemen, I'm Mona, and I'll be your guide for the next tour in about five minutes. Please be ready to go." The matronly woman never cracked a smile during her announcement.

Dee Dee turned around and whispered, "Who took her teddy bear? She looks like she's been sucking on lemons." She puckered her lips in a mocking expression.

"Play nice, Dee," I cautioned, but I couldn't help giggling.

We followed her out of the gift shop into a small garden area. Mona started her spiel about the house. I positioned my camera to take a shot.

She stared straight at me. "Ma'am!"

I pointed my finger toward my chest and shrugged my shoulders.

"Yes, you. There is no photography during the tour. Did you not see the sign in the gift shop?" All eyes turned toward me.

I felt my face turning red. "No ma'am, I guess I didn't." *Geeze louise, you don't have to be so rude about it.*

We entered the house and I pulled out a pen and tablet to take notes since I couldn't shoot photographs. Before I could make my first stroke I heard that authoritative voice again.

"Ma'am!"

I glanced up, hoping she wasn't talking to me. No such luck.

"You can't take notes in here."

I guess Dee Dee had enough of her rudeness and decided to call her on it. "Well, just why can't we take pictures *or* notes?" She put her hands on her hips, mimicking Mona's stance. Under her breath I heard her say, "It's not like this house is top secret or anything."

Mona's eyes grew round and her face turned pink. Her reaction made me wonder if anyone had ever questioned her authority. She sputtered before giving Dee Dee a response. "Just because we don't."

Wow, that's the best reason I've ever heard. I discretely nudged Dee Dee. "Don't worry about it. I'll memorize what I need." Her glazed stare and open mouth indicated she doubted my recall skills. I smiled encouragement, anxious to get the attention off of us.

We walked through several rooms filled with valuable antiques and pictures. Our sober tour guide gave a detailed history and description of every artifact. No one could claim they didn't get their money's worth. We headed toward Mr. William's office when a disembodied voice from the back yelled out, "Isn't this where Williams bit the dust?"

CHAPTER THIRTY-TWO

I heard a sharp intake of breath. "We don't talk about that here," Mona exclaimed. I found it ironic that talk about the infamous murder wasn't allowed. The book and movie, *Midnight in the Garden of Good and Evil*, had made Jim Williams and his love of restoring homes famous. The rest of the tour went quickly. We were ushered out of the house as fast as Mona could get us out.

Throughout the tour a uniformed man had followed us through the house. He held back a few feet behind the group, but it was obvious he was a security guard.

"Dee, I think that might be Bert. Let's see if we can get a look at his name tag."

"Okay." In perfect Dee Dee style she skipped the investigation and went right in for the kill. "Hi, is your name Bert Watkins?"

"How may I help you?"

Dee Dee turned and smiled at me. "The balls' in your court."

"Bert, is there somewhere private we can talk? I work for *Georgia By the Way* and I'd like to interview you about the Mercer Williams House." I sent up a silent prayer. *Father, I need your help here.*

Bert swallowed and his Adam's apple bobbled up and down. "Well, we aren't allowed to talk about the murder." I swanny I thought I saw him shake. Was he that afraid of Mona?

"That's all right. We don't have to talk about the dastardly deed. I'll focus on the house and the antiques Mr. Williams amassed." Maybe Dee Dee would bring it up later.

He surveyed the gift shop before he answered. "I guess it won't hurt to talk to you for a while. Follow me to my office." I could have hugged him, but I restrained my impulse. I hoped we could escape before Attila the Hun returned to announce the next tour. We wove our way through tourists and exited out the back door of the gift shop. We stopped in the doorway of what appeared to be a tool shed. Bert turned around and looked at Dee Dee like he'd just noticed she'd tagged along.

He eyed Dee Dee up and down. "Uh, my office is kinda' small. I'm not sure we can all fit in there."

A spark of fire lit up Dee Dee's eyes. I hurried to extinguish it before she squashed this little man into a pancake.

"It's okay; this won't take long." I had my own doubts, but didn't dare voice them. Dee Dee and I both weighed more than Grace's ex-husband. I could see where he would be an easy target for a strong willed woman. I didn't know how he managed to snag a job as a security guard.

He didn't look too convinced we'd fit, but he led the way into the cramped tool shed. Off to the left was a small area with a desk and chair. He was right; we couldn't fit in the confined area. Dee Dee stood among the rakes and shovels, but I needed her with me. As always, I kept my promise to ask questions for the magazine. Then I loaded for bear.

"Do you know Grace Watkins?" I mentally braced myself for his reply.

His brows rose. "What has she got to do with the Mercer Williams house?"

"Well she doesn't really have anything to do with it."

"We're here on Laura Walker's behalf," Dee Dee picked up the trail. "She's a person of interest in Grace's murder."

I made finger quotes when Dee Dee said, "person of interest."

He looked from one of us to the other. "Well, there ain't much to tell. We just didn't get along, that's all." Like most other men, Bert seemed to be a man of few words. We'd have to pull them out.

Dee Dee snorted. When we both looked at her she covered her mouth and coughed. *Nice try Dee, but I can see right through that fake cough.*

She went on with the questioning. "Bert, could you tell us some names of people Grace had a run-in with?" Dee Dee grabbed the notebook and pen from my hand.

"I'm sorry ma'am, but it would be easier to name the people she didn't have trouble with. Grace just rubbed people the wrong way. I tried, I truly did, but I couldn't take her nagging at me anymore. It was hard to start over, but I didn't have a choice. I knew if I stayed in the marriage one of us wasn't going to make it out alive." Bert busied himself straightening some papers on his desk, but not before I noticed moisture in his eyes.

"I wish I could have been more help. I need to get back to work now." He stood and swung his hand toward the door, an invitation for us to leave.

"Thanks for your time, Bert." We trailed him out of the tool shed.

We made a few purchases in the gift shop then decided to find somewhere to eat. "I saw a café about a block from here. I think I could walk if you want to."

"Sure, I'm up for a vigorous walk." Dee Dee slung her bag's strap over her shoulder.

"Dee, you know I can't walk fast." I wondered if she'd lost her mind.

She put her arm around my shoulder. "Aw, Trix, I was just kidding. You should have me figured out by now." Her laughter floated through the air.

"I'm just beginning to learn who I am. And I have you and Beau to thank for that. You've encouraged me to look inside myself and find who was in there beside just a mother and wife. Your faith has taught me to lean on the One who is stronger than me. Someone who'll never let me down. Like you know who." Tears dampened my eyes. But this time, instead of sad tears, they were tears of relief. I swiped at the moisture pooled in the corner of my eyes.

Dee Dee squeezed my hand. "I love you, too, Trixie." She rewarded me with a huge smile. "Come on, let's go get something to eat; we're getting way too maudlin."

It felt good to laugh. But we wouldn't be laughing by the end of the day.

CHAPTER THIRTY-THREE

As we walked to the café, a chill invaded my body. I shivered and fast rubbed my arms. I didn't know whether the chill was from the slight breeze that blew or was a forewarning. I decided it was the draft and put it out of my mind. When I later recalled that fateful day, I realized I should have given my gut feeling more credence.

"Trix, take a gander at these houses. They're so beautiful." Dee Dee twirled around to take in all sights.

"Wouldn't you love to live here? Do you ever wonder what the owners do for a living to be able to afford such a house?"

I looked in awe, and yes a bit of envy, at the grand houses surrounding the Mercer Williams house. I noticed most of them boasted ironwork of some kind. Fences, balconies, window boxes, and even rails attached to curved stairways were made of iron.

"I sure do. I sometimes have an urge to ring their doorbell and ask them." She giggled at her comment. "Hey, why don't we just go ahead and do it? I think I'll march up to this house right here and ask for a tour." She pointed to the house in front of us.

My heart skipped a beat. I wasn't sure if she was serious or being facetious. I decided to turn the tables. I grabbed her arm. "Okay, let's go." I headed toward the curved stairway, dragging her along. Her wide eyes and O-shaped mouth told me all I needed to know. I bent over in laughter.

"Trixie! How could you?" She playfully hit me with her enormous bag. "I guess you learned from the best. Come on; I see the café over on the next block."

We discussed what we'd learned from Bert. We agreed he'd confirmed what everyone else had told us; Grace didn't make friends easily. We settled in at the little café on the corner, aptly named The Corner Café. Up-scale tourist trinkets filled a hutch against one of the walls. Homemade jellies, commemorative plates, and candles were just a few of the gifts the diners could buy for their friends left behind at home.

I decided to eat a salad so I wouldn't feel so guilty for all of the calorie-laden food I'd eaten over the last several days. I didn't suppose I would be considered over weight, but it wouldn't take much to push me over the line. I really tried to eat healthy, but I usually failed miserably.

Dee Dee ordered a salad, too. "Hey copy-cat," I said. I shot her a smile to let her know I was kidding.

"Well, they say the greatest compliment is imitation. I thought it was a great idea. Then we can order dessert and feel good about our healthy lunch."

I waggled my fork. "What suggestions do you have for our next move?" I felt like the weight of the world sat on my shoulders. Mama and Laura had put a lot of faith in my crime-solving skills. But the fact was I didn't believe I had special skills. I couldn't have solved the murder in Dahlonega without the help of God and Dee Dee. I needed their help now more than ever.

"Let's go back to the inn and look over our notes. We can get our costumes while we're out for the festival tonight. I'm so excited; I feel like a kid going to the carnival."

"Yeah, I imagine Nana will be acting like a kid tonight." If truth be told, at times I was envious of Nana's ability to tackle life with such exuberance.

Dee Dee's patience with Nana was nothing short of a miracle. "Don't worry, be happy Trix. It'll be all right." She wiped her mouth and reapplied her cherry red lipstick.

We spent the time on the way back to Tybee Island going over the suspects.

I was beginning to lose hope, and recalled that Laura mentioned finding an attorney. Maybe it was time; she was certainly still the prime suspect, even on our list. She had opportunity and motive. Grace made Laura's life miserable. The murder weapon belonged to Laura and her fingerprints covered it. Not good. We had to find someone who had a greater motive than Laura. I told Dee Dee as much.

"I wish we knew more about that bracelet." Out came the infamous tablet and pen. "And what about Bert, and Grace's attempts to control him?"

"But he's been gone for a long time, and he's hardly the bracelet wearing type. There wouldn't be a need for him to kill her now; he seemed fairly content. Unless there's something we don't know about. I think he needs to be toward the bottom." I remembered how controlling Wade could be. He wanted to know where I was and what I was doing.

"Let's go over the names of the guests at Seaside Cottage. There's us, of course." Dee Dee gave a little snort. "What about Ellie Sloan? She seems kind of harmless."

"That might be true, but remember we saw her talking with John Porter and she said she wasn't acquainted with him before they met here. And the Daniels saw them downtown together that first night. I don't know why she would lie about it. I think we need to move her toward the top."

"Okay, she's been moved." Dee Dee punched me in the arm. "Stop!"

"What in the world?" I sputtered. I pulled over, alarmed maybe I'd hit something and didn't see it.

CHAPTER THIRTY-FOUR

I want to take some pictures of the boats," Dee Dee indicated to the harbor. "Wouldn't they make great photos? I could frame them and sell them in the shop. Customers grab up anything to do with the ocean."

I pulled up to the road leading to the docks, next to the bridge on the way to Tybee. I had to admit the old fishing boats made great scenes. I grabbed my camera from the back seat and followed Dee Dee. We spent the next fifteen minutes snapping prize winners.

When we returned to the car we continued our conversation about the list. "Okay, Ellie was last. How about the Daniels, Cassie and Harold? That Cassie's so sweet."

"She sure is. I don't see how she and Harold stay together. He's one of the grouchiest old men I've had the displeasure to meet." I turned on the wipers as large drops of rain splattered on my windshield. "But I don't think they have any motive for murder."

"I think you're right. I forgot about Louise, but I can't imagine her killing a bug." Dee Dee checked out her pictures on her camera's tiny screen as we drove.

"Okay, start on the list for Ocean View."

"George is next on the list. What are your thoughts on the gentleman extraordinaire?"

"What's not to like about him? He's handsome, a perfect gentleman, smart, and Nana loves him," I said. "I can't forget about the night he took off with the bracelet. Now that was just weird."

"That leaves Bubba, Nick and KiKi Sanderson, and John Porter."

"Well I hate to say it, but I don't know why any of them would want to kill Grace. The one that concerns me is John Porter. And that's because he met up with Ellie. I would like to know what they've been up to." I looked over to see the sign for Fort Pulaski, a Civil War fortress. I would have loved to get some pictures, but the rain was really driving down now, and I felt we needed to focus on exonerating Laura. "Who's next?"

"We still have Mary Sue Bartlett and Edna Jackson. If you ask me, Mary Sue is carrying a grudge bigger than my bootie. And that's saying a lot, if you know what I mean." Dee Dee laughed at her own joke.

"I'm not touching that one with a ten-foot pole. But you're right; Mary Sue has a lot of baggage from dealing with Grace. She suffered quite a few losses at Grace's doings. She lost her job, her home, and her dignity. We need to consider her highly as a suspect." I liked Mary Sue and it would disappoint me if she were involved in Grace's murder. But I'd learned that *nice* people could commit murder.

"Then there's Edna. I believe if I had to live with Grace for as long as she has, I might have been tempted to strangle her myself."

"Edna has the patience of Job." Every time I'd say this I'd think about Job and the hand he was dealt. He was often used an example of patience. And it was true he had never cursed God as his wife wanted him to, but he had cursed the day he was born. God hadn't been too happy with him, either. God's booming voice asked Job, "Where were you when I made the foundations of the earth?" Job had changed his attitude right quick. But what I loved about Job was how he was human, just like we were. He had fussed and groused about the things that were happening in his life, just like us; and God still blessed him in the end.

"Hey, Trix!"

I came back from my musings ƴnd looked over at Dee Dee.

"Where did you go?"

"Sorry, what were you saying?"

"I said Edna might not be as patient as we've given her credit for. She might be someone else we need to keep a close eye on." Dee Dee scooted around in her seat. "Good thing we'll be back to the inn shortly." She slapped her backside with her hand and released a hearty laugh. This time I laughed with her.

"I think that covers just about everybody we've talked to. Is there anybody we left out?"

She took a minute to study the list. "We haven't mentioned Jasmine." She held up the notebook and pointed to a name with her pen. "Now there's a scorned woman. I'll never understand why Grace made it her life mission to make other people miserable."

"Well, we'll never get the answer now." I shook my head in bewilderment. I was as stumped as Dee Dee. Why would anyone enjoy making enemies? "Jasmine must have been furious when Grace brought up her past. The question is, was she furious enough to kill her?"

We pulled into Laura's driveway. "Come on; we've talked enough about death and murder. How about we take the evening off and have a great time at the pirate's festival." Dee Dee helped me retrieve all our stuff from the car and lug it in the house.

Nana met us at the door. "I thought you'd never get back. We have to go get our pirate costumes for tonight." She had her jacket hung over one arm and her pocketbook strapped over the other.

CHAPTER THIRTY-FIVE

Whoa there, Nana. Let us catch our breath and we'll go pick out something to wear." Mama walked in the room. "Are you going with us?"

"No thanks, sweetie. I think I'll stay here with Laura. She's really down in the dumps. I don't want to leave her. I imagine most everyone will be downtown tonight." Talk about having the patience of Job. If anyone symbolized patience it was Mama. How she dealt with Nana day in and day out mystified me. Then again, I knew Mama was a firm believer of prayer and spent a lot of time, metaphorically speaking, on her knees.

I threw my arm around her shoulders and gave her a squeeze. Mama had been my saving grace since I was a child. Where Daddy expected perfection, Mama knew perfection was impossible to achieve. When Wade left me and I was drowning in hurt and sorrow, she lifted me up and helped me out of the quicksand of despair. I was so thankful God saw fit to put us together.

I went up to my room and spent a few minutes in front of the mirror. I didn't realize vacations could take so much out of you. I'd have to go home to rest. But then I remembered when I got home Beau would be expecting me to answer the important question. I'd be ready.

I had lain down across the bed to rest my knee for a few minutes, when the next thing I knew Dee Dee was shaking me. "Hey, come on and get up. We've got to hurry if we're going to town."

I reached toward the ceiling. "I could stretch a mile if I didn't have to walk back."

Dee Dee and I laughed until tears were rolling down our cheeks. I know, it wasn't that funny, but we needed the comedic relief. The stress had been palpable.

"Come on; let's get this over with. No telling what Nana will choose to wear. I'm afraid she's going straight for the wench's dress." We arrived at the costume store to discover we weren't the only ones who'd waited until the fifth hour.

I had to admit surprise when Nana came out in the cutest outfit. She had on black pants, a maroon vest, and a white blouse with ruffled sleeves. Black boots adorned her feet.

"Oh, Nana, you look so precious."

She jabbed her hand on her boney hip and swung her fake sword around. "Arr, matey! Lady pirates are not precious."

I'd been chastised. "Yes, ma'am." Dee Dee and I decided to go with suits similar to Nana's, but we didn't look nearly as cute as she did.

We drove back to Seaside Cottage where Louise had set a table fit for a king. Fresh lobster tail, shrimp with garlic butter, cole slaw, asparagus, red potatoes, crab cakes, corn on the cob, and salad. We decided to wait and eat downtown.

All the guests were there and everyone, except Mama and Laura, had plans to attend the festival. By the time we arrived downtown the festivities had begun. Gaily dressed pirates danced in the street, swaying rhythmically to the music. The crowded street ran parallel to the beach. I looked across the parking lot and listened to the waves lapping gently onto the beach. I stood in awe at the magnificent sight.

Nana tugged on my sleeve. "Come on, Trixie, let's get some action. I'm supposed to meet George in a little while, but I want to try some of the food while we wait." I shot a glance at Dee Dee. She shoulder shrugged and raised her eyebrows.

"Nana you eat like a bird – all the time." Our laughter faded in the midst of the noise. Though Nana stood with her hands on her hips, her face wore a grin. The mood was light and smiles adorned the faces of the festival-goers. Caught up in the excitement, I found it hard to believe I'd been reluctant to come.

We fought our way from booth to booth until Nana chose a corndog. I watched in bewilderment as she slathered mustard on the cornmeal coated hotdog and took a big bite. Dee Dee and I opted for a hamburger.

Dee Dee shook a french fry at Nana. "Now when are you supposed to meet George?"

Through a mouthful, Nana mumbled. "We're supposed to meet at Pirate's Treasure around seven."

I reached over and wiped off a smudge of mustard on the corner of her mouth. "Well, we'd better hurry because it's fifteen 'till. It'll take us a few minutes to walk over there."

I was surprised to see Ellie Sloan and John Porter in front of the store when we arrived.

Ellie spoke first. "Hi. Having a good time?"

John pulled off his pirate hat, bent over and swept his hat in a broad greeting. Somehow I'd never pictured him as a gentleman. I still didn't. If Ellie and John didn't know each other then why did they keep showing up together? "Hi, ladies. Are you looking for George?"

"Yes," Nana said, "have you seen him?" Her eyes surveyed the surroundings.

"We sure have," John said. "He said he had an errand he needed to take care of, so we told him to go ahead and we'd keep you company until he got back."

Ellie nodded her head in agreement.

"Go ahead, Trixie. I'll be all right." Nana bounced with excitement.

I had a gut feeling not to leave Nana, but I didn't follow it. I would pay for that mistake.

CHAPTER THIRTY-SIX

We walked toward the booths now lining every square inch of the beach parking lot. "Think Nana will be okay?"

"Sure," Dee Dee said. "George will be there in a little while."

We browsed around makeshift shops filled with every imaginable Savannah and Tybee Island memorabilia. Several vendors sold pirate costumes and were doing a hardy business. Aromas of food, seawater, and crowds floated in the air. The sides of the tents flapped in a cool ocean breeze. The midway, filled with laughter and "Ahoy, mateys," bore witness to the exciting atmosphere of the festival.

"Look, Trix! There's a booth selling homemade ice-cream. Let's get some," Dee Dee said.

We opted for chocolate-chocolate chip, which could possibly result in our death by chocolate —what a way to go. We sat on a bench and people-watched while we deliberated over *the list*. There were a variety of costumes: men pirates, lady pirates, and more than a fair share of wenches.

"You know. I'm so glad Nana didn't decide to wear a wench's costume. Not that she'd even have enough to fill out the top." Images of Nana in the hot pink bathing suit flashed through my mind. I'd never be able to look at a pink bikini the same.

"Speaking of Nana, is it time to meet up with her?" Dee Dee stuck the last bite of her cone in her mouth and licked her fingers. "Yummy."

I looked at my watch. We told Nana we'd meet back at the General

Store at nine and then we could hang out with her and George. "Yep, it's almost nine. Let's head over that way." I ran my tongue over my lips in an effort to lick off some of the sticky.

We blazed a trail through the wall of people. I didn't panic when I couldn't spot Nana right off. I figured they were somewhere inside. We looked around several minutes. When Nana and George didn't show, my heart thudded against my chest.

"Where are they, Dee Dee?" I didn't recognize my voice as it was a couple octaves higher than usual.

She grabbed my arm. "Look! There's Ellie and John over in the corner. She's waving at us." We hot-footed it in their direction. "I bet they know where Nana and George are." Dee Dee shoved pirates out of the way to make a path for us.

"Oh, I'm so glad to see y'all. We can't find Nana and George. They were supposed to meet us here and we thought you might know where they are." John leaned in toward me. I figured he just wanted to get close so I could hear him.

He grabbed my arm and I felt something hard against my back. His hot breath tickled my neck and I could smell pizza on his breath. "Don't move or make a sound. I've got a gun on you."

"Why?"

"You know why," John spat out the words.

"No, I don't know why." I looked over my shoulder and came face to face with my nemesis.

"If you want to see your *Nana* alive you'll come with me quietly."

"What about Dee Dee?" I wondered if we'd discovered the killers. If they didn't take Dee Dee she could go for help.

"Ellie has your friend. Do you think I'm stupid enough to let her go?" Well, I was hoping he was. "We are going to walk out to my car and you'd better not make a scene. You'll never see her alive again."

The pain in my rib convinced me he meant business. All I wanted to do was get to Nana and make sure she was all right. *Lord, let Nana be okay and protect us from evil.* We made our way to a small car. My mind whirled with ways to overtake John and make a run for it. He threw a tow sack over any ideas I might have had when he ordered me into the driver's seat.

Ellie shoved Dee Dee in the back seat and got in with her. John directed me in what seemed to be circles. I wondered if he was trying to throw us off-course. We drove down a long sandy driveway that ended near the beach. A bungalow stood among a grove of palm trees.

"We are going to go in nice and easy. I don't want to shoot you."

Well don't, then.

"We don't want you to shoot us either." Dee Dee said what I only had the courage to think.

John showed me where to stop the car, and we all got out, stumbling in the darkness.

"Shut up and keep moving," he shoved me forward when I tripped on a root. A small shack loomed up, and I groped up the steps inside. And then I heard her before I saw her. Grunts and groans emanated from somewhere in the semi-darkness.

"Nana!" As my eyes adjusted to the dim light I saw her tied to a chair, duct tape covered her mouth. "Are you all right?" I broke free from John's grasp and headed over to her.

"She's all right. And don't try anything funny." John waved his gun in the air like it was connected to a ceiling fan. Ellie stood with feet apart and she held her gun sideways like a member of a street gang. One mystery was solved – they did indeed know each other before coming to Savannah.

Dee Dee's eyes, wide with fear or maybe disbelief, reminded me of a deer caught in headlights.

"I guess y'all killed Grace." Dee Dee stated the obvious.

John bellowed a maniacal laugh. "Yeah, I killed her."

Ellie spoke up. "Hey, babe, don't tell them anything." She pointed her gun toward a bed beside Nana. "Get over there and sit down."

"Don't worry about what they know. They won't be around long enough to say anything."

CHAPTER THIRTY-SEVEN

Ummm. Ummm." Nana tried her best to speak.

"Can't you remove the tape?" Shock rattled me when he walked over to Nana and ripped off the tape as fast as he could. Nana squealed in pain.

John laughed. "Well, you asked me to take it off. And don't get any ideas about screaming, because I'll shoot you faster than you can blink."

We knew who killed Grace, but why? If I could keep them talking, maybe George would send for help. Then again, where did George fit into this scenario? He appeared to be a good guy, but why did he know so much about the bracelet Captain Jack found. Was he a jewel thief? Was he involved with Ellie and John?

I sat beside Nana and held her hand. "Why did you bring us out here?"

Dee Dee sat beside me.

"Oh, please. You know why." John looked at us like we were aliens.

I really didn't know for sure. I thought maybe they felt the heat of mine and Dee Dee's questioning and wanted to get us out of the way, but the way he was posturing, I didn't want to upset him anymore.

"I'll go along with your little ruse. We know you work for International Insurance. Nobody would act as goofy as you two women if you weren't putting on an act. And y'all were going around asking everybody questions. We saw right through it."

"Hey, watch it. That's my niece you're calling goofy," Nana said.

"Shut up old lady. You want me to slap some tape back on your mouth?" Nana didn't answer, but she shot pure fire from her eyes. If those lasers were real he'd have been obliterated right on the spot.

Ellie joined in the fracas. "We knew when Captain Jack discovered the bracelet you'd figure out we'd lifted the jewels. We knew you'd come if we had your Nana. It worked, too, didn't it honey?" She looked like a fox with a mouth full of feathers.

I tried to piece together this bizarre puzzle. They were jewel thieves being chased by an insurance detective. John thought we were the investigators. They had recognized the bracelet, so it must have been from their stash. How did Grace tie in with international burglars? My mantra became, keep them talking, keep them talking.

"I'm sure you realize any self-respecting insurance company will be keeping track of our every move." I decided to play along and buy us some time. "You'd be a fool to hurt us."

Dee Dee plunged ahead while Ellie and John exchanged glances, considering my dare. "And what did Grace ever do to deserve a death sentence?"

John snorted. "She snooped where she shouldn't have. She stumbled on the stash of jewels we hid in our room and then tried to blackmail me. She might have been used to terrifying others with her bossiness, but she met her match in me. Nobody is going to threaten me and get away with it. So I lured her out to the beach, took the gnome, and used it as a weapon. It was a perfect plan. Until that bracelet turned up. I thought I'd recovered all the pieces she'd taken."

"They'll be here soon looking for us." Dee Dee scooted around on the couch.

"Nobody is going to find us here," John said. "Now, stop moving around and keep your hands in front of you or I'll tie you all up."

I don't know how long we sat there while John and Ellie discussed our fates in hushed tones. I hoped we'd planted some doubts in their minds. I squeezed Nana's hand.

"All right, I'm going to go out for a while and I'm leaving Ellie to guard you. You'd better enjoy your last few minutes on this earth, because when I get back you're going to meet your maker."

My stomach constricted and my heart palpitated. Maybe he was going out for a silencer. I could feel the sweat trickle down my forehead. A stray drop of sweat burned my eye. I reached up to wipe it off. *Dear God, help us out of this terrible situation. Not that I don't want to meet you, but I've got things I need to take care of first. And please hurry!*

They say God works in mysterious ways, and what happened in the next few minutes was a testimony to the truth of that statement. John had tied Nana to a straight back chair with her hands and feet clasped together with zip ties. I can't imagine the fear she must have felt when they trussed her up like a Thanksgiving turkey.

When John's footsteps clomped down the steps, Nana donned a pitiful face. "These ties are cutting into my skin. Can't you loosen them up some?"

"All right, but you better not try anything funny. I'm going to cut them off and if anybody makes a move their as good as shot." Ellie scrounged around until she found a wicked looking pair of scissors. She reached to cut the plastic band and the next thing I knew Dee Dee had moved with the grace of a cat, or maybe an elephant. She took the purse I'd never make fun of again, reared back like a discus thrower, and with one fell swoop brought it down on Ellie's back.

Startled, Ellie let out a blood-curdling scream and fell to the floor and the gun landed close to Nana's now untied hands. She grabbed it up, and boggled it like a hot potato. It flew up in the air and landed next to me on the bed. With the calmness of a sane person I picked it up and mimicked the stance Ellie took earlier with my legs apart and the gun pointed straight at her.

Dee Dee smoothed out her pirate's costume as if she were ready to make her debut on the runway. She looked at Ellie and smirked. "Now whose court is the ball in?" That's my Dee Dee. My heart strummed in my chest and I struggled to keep my arms up. The gun was heavy and cold in my hands.

Before a stunned Ellie had a chance to act, the door burst open and a bevy of blue-uniformed SWAT officers swarmed in. One of them took the gun as I lowered it, and then someone yelled the all clear. The sea of blue opened up and I was never so glad to see anyone than I was to see Detective Baker striding toward me. It was all I could do to resist giving the burly guy a great big hug.

CHAPTER THIRTY-EIGHT

With the arrival of help, my adrenaline waned and my brave persona dissipated. As my knees buckled, Detective Baker caught me, and the next thing I knew George and Dee Dee were helping me to the couch.

Nana squealed, "George, I knew you'd find me."

"You better believe it. I wasn't going to let anything happen to my new friend." He gave her a wink.

The policemen released Nana from the chair while others hand-cuffed Ellie. Seems what goes around comes around. Now she'd know what it felt like to have her hands bound. As we followed them outside, I saw that John was already sitting in the backseat of a patrol unit.

"How? Why? What happened?" My shattered nerves prevented me from stringing together a coherent sentence.

Dee Dee didn't do much better when she tried to speak. "Yeah, what she said."

Detective Baker signed something on a clipboard for one of the uniformed officers, and turned to us. "Ladies, you've just helped us nab a couple of international jewel thieves."

Nana spoke up. "And they killed Grace. I heard them talking about the murder. We all did." George stood beside Nana with his hand on her shoulder while she rubbed her numb wrists.

"We know," Detective Baker said.

I couldn't help feeling a bit smug that he had more respect for us now.

"They had this crazy notion we're insurance investigators. I guess because we were asking the guests questions about the murder." Detective Baker's brow raised, but he only shook his head at my confession.

"They weren't too far off." George's next words surprised me. He shot me a huge smile. "You see, I'm the insurance investigator. I work for International Insurance Company and I've been following this pair for several weeks now. They've been hitting tourist towns and then moving on to their next destination."

"When you disappeared from the festival, he alerted me, and we put out a BOLO for you and their car." Detective Baker said. We all turned to John's car sitting under a live oak.

"I told you George was on the up and up," Nana said.

George laughed. "I know you had doubts about me, Trixie. It was easy to tell you suspected there was more to me than being just another tourist. I'm sorry I had to be so evasive, but I didn't want to blow my cover. As soon as I arrived in town I let Detective Baker know who I was."

"So he was in on it from the beginning?" Thoughts swirled in my head like water swirling around a drain.

The Detective picked up from there. "Yes, he was. As soon as George told us about them we gave him the go ahead to continue his investigation as long as he kept us in the loop."

Dee Dee interrupted the detective with a question I had on my mind. "Is Laura off the hook now they've confessed to murdering Grace?"

The first sincere smile I'd seen on Detective Baker's face appeared. "Yes she is. I'm sorry she had to go through the traumatic experience, but I had to do my job until the evidence was gathered. These two have gotten away too many times, and we couldn't risk losing them again. When the cat found that bracelet, we had another direction to go and almost enough evidence to connect the murder to the stolen jewels. Their kidnapping you and confessing will make the D.A. very happy."

Nana asked George the next question. "How did you find us?" She reached up and patted the hand on her shoulder. She looked so little and frail. Her tenacity often made me forget just how fragile she was. I wiped a tear, so thankful nothing had happened to her. Even though she was a little spitfire to be reckoned with, I shuddered to think what my life would be like without her.

"When I discovered you'd left with a young couple, I knew they'd taken you. I drove straight to Detective Baker. I'd already put a tracking device on their car so I knew we could pick up where they were. The detective called for backup from the Savannah Police. We arrived just a few minutes before John came out. He walked right into the hands of his captors."

Detective Baker barked, "Get 'em out of here."

In my hysteria I thought of a line from Hawaii Five-O, "Book 'em, Dano."

We'd called ahead and let Mama and Laura know what had happened and that we'd be home after we gave our statements. They ran out to meet us when we arrived.

"Nana, I'm so glad you weren't hurt." Mama hugged Nana with one arm and me with the other. Dee Dee circled in and we laughed, cried, and laughed some more before beetling over to the couch to go over everything that had happened.

We stayed in town another day to answer more questions for Detective Baker, giving our formal statements, promising to let him know if we recalled anything later we might have forgotten.

Living through a life and death situation makes you see the future in a different way. It was almost like everything was so beautiful it was in 3-D. I returned to Vans Valley knowing without a doubt I wanted to become Mrs. Beau Beaumont.

We decided to have a Christmas wedding.

John and Ellie were charged with Grace Watkins' murder. George became a hero with his insurance company. There were many happy jewelry owners who gave their thanks to George. He and Nana are corresponding and making plans to meet at a future date.

In a twist of fate, Grace had left a legacy. When the lawyers read her will, no one was more surprised than Edna because Grace left her Ocean View Inn. All those years working for Grace and enduring her tyranny paid off for Edna. The first thing she did was hire Mary Sue Bartlett to help run the bed and breakfast with the promise of a significant pay raise, a room for her daughter and herself, and the promise she could develop recipes to her heart's content. The buzz is that they are releasing a cookbook with all of Mary Sue's specialties to start a college fund for Sarah Joe.

Since I had been officially on vacation, Harv didn't expect me to write an article about Savannah or Tybee Island. However, I knew with Savannah's rich history I'd be able to write an award-winning article. I took extra time with it, and when I turned it in to him, Harv was thrilled. He ran it as a feature, and when "Turtles and Tourism are only the Tip of the Talk in Tybee" won the Silver Award at the Excellence Awards Gala sponsored by the Magazine and Publishing Association of Georgia, I finally felt like I'd lived up to my title as a historical magazine writer.

Beau and I would love for y'all to attend our wedding. And bring your appetite, because we're featuring several of Mary Sue's world famous dishes.

• The verse Trixie chose for "Terror on Tybee Island" is: Look at the birds of the air; they do not sow or reap or store away in barns, and yet your heavenly Father feeds them. Are you not much more valuable than they? Matthew 6:26 (NIV). What is your favorite verse?

• Betty Jo, Trixie's mother, talks her and Dee Dee into helping her friend Laura when she becomes the main suspect in a murder case. Trixie was hesitant, but decided she would want someone to do the same for her. Have you found yourself in a situation where you didn't want to help in the beginning but you were glad you did? Do you ever ask yourself "Wouldn't I want someone to do the same for me?"

• Trixie was sure Nana's new friend, George, might be up to no good. It turns out that not only is he a good guy, but he saved their lives. Have you ever jumped to conclusion about someone and then found out you had misjudged them? Do you have an example?

• Nana is a little spit-fire. She is not going to sit in a rocking chair just because she has a little age on her. Do you know a Nana or have a Nana in your life? Have they done something funny or embarrassing?

• What is your favorite scene? Why?

• Who is your favorite character? Why?